Ghosts

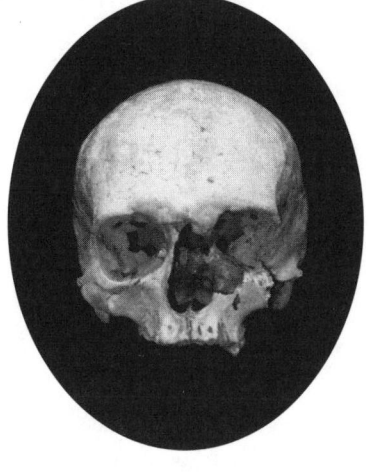

Ed Okonowicz

Ghosts
First Edition

Copyright 2001 by Edward M. Okonowicz Jr.
All rights reserved.

ISBN 1-890690-08-2

No portion of this book may be reproduced, in any form,
except for brief passages for review purposes,
without written permission from the author.

Published by
Myst and Lace Publishers, Inc.
1386 Fair Hill Lane
Elkton, Maryland 21921

www.mystandlace.com

Printed in the U.S.A.
by Victor Graphics

Layout, Typography and Cover Design
by Kathleen Okonowicz

Dedications

To our proofreaders, listed below, John, Barbara,
Marianna, Sue, Ted and Monica.
Their fine work is so important and appreciated.
Ed Okonowicz

To Geraldine McKeown, my friend and mentor.
You have opened up a whole new world for me.
Kathleen Burgoon Okonowicz

Acknowledgments

The author and illustrator appreciate
the assistance of those
who have played an important role
in this project, including

John Brennan

Barbara Burgoon

Marianna Dyal

Sue Moncure

Ted Stegura and

Monica Witkowski,

for their proofreading and suggestions.

Special thanks are extended to Patty Cannon, whose skull,
currently resting in a hatbox in the Dover, Delaware, Public Library,
is featured on the cover of this book.

Also available from Myst and Lace Publishers, Inc.

Spirits Between the Bays Series

Volume I
Pulling Back the Curtain

Volume II
Opening the Door

Volume III
Welcome Inn

Volume IV
In the Vestibule

Volume V
Presence in the Parlor

Volume VI
Crying in the Kitchen

Volume VII
Up the Back Stairway

Volume VIII
Horror in the Hallway

Volume IX
Phantom in the Bedchamber

DelMarVa Murder Mystery Series

FIRED!

Halloween House

Stairway over the Brandywine
A Love Story

Possessed Possessions
Haunted Antiques, Furniture and Collectibles

Possessed Possessions 2
More Haunted Antiques, Furniture and Collectibles

Disappearing Delmarva
Portraits of the Peninsula People

Terrifying Tales of the Beaches and Bays

Ghosts

Table of Contents

Introduction
Why Do We Read This Stuff?   1

True Stories

University Avenue Ghost House   4
Newark, Delaware

A Short Ride from the Hancock House   15
Salem County, New Jersey

Haunted Barns   20
On Delmarva and in New Jersey

Only a Coincidence   26
Somewhere on Delmarva

Ghostly Guardian Angel   30
Philadelphia, Pennsylvania

House Ghost   37
Lewes, Delaware

Short Sightings   40
Abandoned Fort on the Atlantic Coast
Talbot County, Maryland
East of Baltimore
North East and Rising Sun, Maryland

Legend and Lore

Ghosts in the Cotton Field   46
Churchville, Georgia
by Jamie Cherundolo

They Buried This Judge Twice in Dover   54
Dover, Delaware

Unending Drive   57
Somewhere in Georgia

Slicer and Snooks   63
Queen Anne's County, Maryland

Preserving the Past   69
New Castle County, Delaware

Not Your Average Old Haunted House   81
Delaware City, Delaware

Introduction

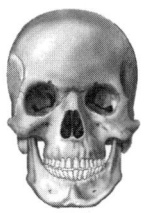

Why Do We Read This Stuff?

From the time I began storytelling, I have been asked to share ghost stories. Whether it's a Mother's Day luncheon at a posh retirement home, a Boy Scouts awards dinner in a church basement, a family Christmas party in a private home or a college admissions program in a modern lecture hall—someone usually will ask: "Do you have a good ghost story?"

Since 1994, I have written 11 books on Mid-Atlantic ghost stories and two volumes about haunted antiques and collectibles. Ninety percent of the stories in these volumes are based on interviews with people who have written letters, called on the phone or stopped to talk after book signings or story programs—so they are the real thing, not folktales or legends.

As a result of my books, I've been associated with ghosts so heavily that even if I wanted to divorce myself from the paranormal it wouldn't be possible. On my desk sit scores of manila folders containing hundreds of leads for chapters in future books—unexplained incidents at haunted inns and restaurants, in spooky theaters, on historic battlefields, near sunken treasure sites and even spirits in vehicles, schools and churches.

I've helped develop ghost tours at Fort Delaware—and at other historic sites. More recently, my historian friend Mike Dixon and I established "History and Haunts," town and cemetery walking tours as fund-raising events for non-profit organizations.

I've attended UFOlogist meetings, met with witches and warlocks, passed the time with gravediggers and undertakers and interviewed a man who is searching for Bigfoot—in eastern Maryland.

Ghosts

My ghostly guides have led me down quite a few paths that I would never have considered. And on some of these lanes (particularly my two books on haunted objects) I was very reluctant to travel.

But the question often arises: Why are people fascinated with death, and the macabre and the unknown?

Movies such as *The Sixth Sense* and *What Lies Beneath?* pack in audiences, and television programs like *The X-Files* attract a devoted following. Attend a party and mention casually that you "know someone" who lives in a haunted house and you most certainly will hear from others who "know of" or who "have experienced" their own mysterious incidents much closer to home (often in the attic, bedroom or cellar). Plus, if they don't have a story of their own, they definitely want to hear more of the juicy details of yours.

Some believe this keen interest in the paranormal is associated with the human need to be frightened, which modern society is unable to provide.

When the settlers arrived in America, wild animals were a serious threat, as were Indians, disease and the natural elements such as weather and geography. Also, there were no reliable supplies of water and food. Medicine was in its infancy and often ineffective. Death from disease and everyday life occurrences, such as work and childbirth, was common, expected and accepted.

Wars—Revolutionary, 1812, Civil—on American soil provided a heavy dose of terror, as did later conflicts, including battles on foreign battlefields. But today military engagements on the American continent are nonexistent. Serious communicable diseases are under control. Most of us do not live in fear of murder, burglary, arson or assault. Modern maps and highways, plus advances in communication technology have made it safe to travel beyond our immediate communities without fear of being lost or eaten in the woods by monsters or wild beasts.

So today, when are we afraid for our lives? How often are we scared to death?

We might become terrified while driving on a highway at 70 miles per hour in a nasty rainstorm or trying to work our way through a thick fog when visibility is poor. In both instances, we are afraid to pull off the road for fear of striking another car. So we white-knuckle it through the trip and pray to God for quick reactions and divine protection.

Other than these incidents, and occasional natural disasters—such as hurricanes, tornadoes, earthquakes and floods—we are safe, and fear is a rare visitor.

To satisfy this human need to be terrified, we seek out books, movies, stories and guided tours that offer a quick dose of fear—as long as we can regroup quickly and laugh off the moment of terror in the company of friends. Certainly, Halloween is the prime season when Father Fright is most visible, but this human thirst for goosebumps and mystery continues year round. Even if we know the ending of a horror story or scary movie, a carefully crafted, creepy tale can still send shivers up our spines.

But we handle these moments of unease because we will return to the security of our home and fall asleep, knowing that talk of "ghosties and ghoulies and long legged beasties" is only make believe and "it could never happen to me."

Right?

Maybe. Who knows for sure?

Many of the events featured in this book happened to people who also thought the spirit world only existed on paper pages and movie screens. They didn't expect to have an up-close encounter with the unexplained or a personal moment of dread.

In some places, above and below the ground, many will swear that the dead are still out there. And on some dark night, when you are alone and unprepared, a spectre may travel your way.

Until we meet again,

Happy Hauntings and, like the Boy Scouts say, be prepared.

Ed Okonowicz
In Fair Hill, Maryland,
at the northern edge
of the Delmarva Peninsula
—Fall 2001

Author's note: This book features "Ghosts in the Cotton Fields," an original story, written by Jamie Cherundolo, of Newark, Delaware, a junior English major at the University of Delaware.

Ghost House on University Avenue

Sometimes you don't have to go far to find a haunted house. It can be a building you've passed hundreds of times—on your ride to work, while going to church, as you head toward a nearby shopping center or make a trip to the mall.

In this case, the haunted residence is an old semi-detached home that was built about 100 years ago. It still stands, on University Avenue in the city limits of Newark, Delaware, but is quite a bit different than it looked a century ago. The paint is peeling, its functional shutters are gone and its side and rear yards have been torn out to make way for the sleek and colorful cars of its transient 21st century college-age renters.

No doubt, several generations ago a single family lived in this three-story frame structure. Excitable children and weary parents slept in the second-floor bedrooms and enjoyed cool glasses of lemonade on the front porch in summer. They ate at a small kitchen table, and, I'm sure, listened to old radio dramas and variety programs during the middle years of the 20th century in their parlor overlooking narrow, gravel-paved University Avenue.

The house was probably built as a home for factory workers, hunched over men who carried metal lunchpails and walked to the nearby paper and fiber mills along the White Clay Creek. Six days a week, they responded to whistle blasts that signaled the start of the morning shift, the beginning and end of lunch and the much anticipated 5 o'clock hour that marked the end of their repetitive workday.

Today the mills are gone, closed up and in the process of being transformed into fancy apartments or trendy boutiques. Family members of the home's first residents have all been carried off in wooden boxes or metal coffins to nearby cemeteries for their eternal rest. And ownership has changed hands several times, but still the house remains. Somehow, the old building has been lucky enough to escape the hazards of fire, the highway engineer's decision to widen the avenue and greedy developer's eye, which could assign it to its ultimate enemy—the wrecker's ball.

Within its creaking frame, this old house knows it can't hold out forever. It will suffer from ill fortune and be gone one day as sure as a lucky gambler's winning streak disappears faster than it materialized.

But thanks to a recent resident, we at least have captured the paranormal events that occurred in the "University Ghost House."

Laura, a former coworker at the University of Delaware, suggested that I call her friend Krazy Kurt. She said he, along with a few friends, had lived in a haunted house while students at the University of Delaware.

I've been working at UD for 20 years and knew that a number of the older properties had been bought up by landlords and turned into student housing, so the prospect that a worn and used building might have some stories associated with it made perfect sense. But I had no idea when I sat down with Kurt, relocated in his modern apartment off Elkton Road, that a single structure—that I had passed every day—would offer such a gold mine of haunted infestation.

I had planned to devote about 45 minutes to Kurt's interview, and we began talking at 8 in the evening. Three hours later, I walked to my car still sensing the remnants of chills that had occurred during our conversation. I was thankful for Laura's suggestion that I get Kurt's story . . . and you will be, too.

In the beginning

Kurt had mentioned something quite a few times during our interview, so I'll state it at the beginning of his story: Kurt is "not a wimp."

Ghosts

At 6' 4 " and 290 pounds, it wasn't the kind of thing he had to mention, and I told him so. Nevertheless, he stressed that he wanted to be sure I, and the readers, knew that there weren't many things that could scare him.

I believed what he said.

In addition to his size, which consumed a good part of his full-size living room couch, Kurt's background was impressive. He was a former University of Delaware football player who had been in the National Football League for nearly two years.

At the time we talked about his ghostly experinces, he was more excited about his first teaching and coaching job. In fact, we spent about 15 minutes discussing his experiences at UD, teaching school and football in general. There were a lot of laughs in that quarter hour.

The mood changed dramatically when we switched the focus of our conversation to ghosts.

"Let me tell you this up front," Kurt said. "There were five guys in this house, all huge football players, no wimps. And we all were very skeptical about ghosts. In other words, we were unbelievers, totally."

And later? I asked.

Kurt smiled, raised his hand and said, "Let me start at the beginning."

He and his teammates had lived in the three-story home for one year, during the mid-1990s. They had heard talk, he said, about strange things happening in other houses in the area, but they didn't pay attention.

"After all," he said, "every house on the block was creepy. They all looked haunted. They needed painting, they had dirt basement floors with stone walls. The floors creaked and the wind blew through the cracks in the windows."

Of course, from the first few days they moved in, strange things started to happen. "But," Kurt admitted, "we didn't put everything together until much later."

Clyde, the clock and the traveling photo

A chocolate Labrador Retriever named Clyde would stare at the corner of the living room ceiling and bark constantly and nothing could make it stop. They even waved thick, juicy steaks in the air to attract it away from where it was barking, but the dog would not stop staring at something no one else could see.

Kurt recalled, "People would come in and say, 'Your dog's crazy!' But that wasn't the case. Clyde was fine, except when he was in that house."

The student sleeping in the first-floor apartment had a problem with his clock. No matter what time he set the alarm for, it would go off at 4:07 in the morning. Each time it occurred, he would reset the alarm, and it would still activate at 4:07 a.m.

"We all thought the clock was broken," Kurt said, "so he threw it out, got a new one. And when he plugged it in the same thing happened. It also went off at 4:07.

"Like I said, we all were skeptical about ghosts," Kurt added, "meaning none of us believed. About this time the guy living on the first floor was getting a little frightened. But it really wasn't that bad for him. He never had anything else other than the clock happen to him."

Kurt paused, took a sip of soda and said, that some of the roommates were starting to get a strange feeling when they were in the house alone. "It was a strange dark and dreadful feeling, but we never shared it with each other at this point."

One of the roommates on the second floor had a baby picture of his girlfriend, when she was one year old, stuck in the edge of his mirror. Suddenly, the picture was missing,

"He would come into the kitchen, really upset, and say, 'I want that picture back! Right now!' But none of us had it. The other guys would tease him and whine, 'Anybody got the picture of his little girl?' And that really set him off. But the thing is, if any of us did it, we would have told the others, because we would be proud of upsetting him. But no one ever admitted doing it."

Each time the picture was missing, a few days later it would reappear, back in its spot in the mirror.

"Now look," Kurt said, "here we were, in this big, dark house with a scary feeling growing worse by now. And we're not talking a bunch of little college girls. We were 270-pound, grown men, football players. But none of us, at this point, had admitted our concerns to everyone else."

Kurt said he told his best friend that living there was beginning to bother him.

"I told him," Kurt said, "I was almost afraid to walk alone from the first floor to my attic room."

His friend replied, "I don't know how you can live in the attic. It's bad enough on the second floor."

Kurt said he admitted, "It's spooky here. But we have to live here, have to stay. It's no big deal."

Screams and night visitors

It was in October, about three months after they had moved in, when things began to move into high gear. One of the roommates on the second floor woke up in the middle of the night, at 3 o'clock in the morning, screaming at the top of his lungs.

"It sounded like someone was getting killed," Kurt said. "I jumped out of my bed. We all went rushing into his room. I remember my first thought, being a football player, was that he probably had a cramp in his calf or leg, or maybe there was someone else in the house.

"When we got there, he was beside himself. The only way to put it was he looked like he had seen a ghost. His face was completely white and he was hyperventilating. He was speechless."

Several of the guys shouted at him, demanding to know the cause of his screams.

"He told us he woke up, but thought he was dreaming," Kurt said. "But there was a young woman floating by his door. He was scared and rubbed his eyes, and then realized he was awake. Then the figure floated through the door and disappeared."

The immediate reaction from his housemates was a combination of laughter and disbelief. Then the teasing began, but that made the victim upset, and he started shouting that "It wasn't a dream!"

One of the other guys tried to explain that he had experienced vivid dreams that almost seem real, while another friend suggested it was the result of something he had eaten.

"We were all trying to rationalize," Kurt said. "We didn't believe what he said could have happened. But he kept saying over and over it wasn't a dream. After about a half-hour of talking to him, I think we convinced him that it really was only a bad dream."

But Kurt and another roommate believed what their friend had told them immediately. They just didn't want anyone else to know how they felt, and they wanted to see how the other housemates would react.

A week later, the same victim, who, Kurt said, was a serious, rational and logical guy, witnessed a second apparition.

It was 3 o'clock in the morning, the same time as the first disturbance, but this time there was shouting and banging.

When the other residents entered the room, he was shaking and pointing up at the ceiling. This time, the night visitor was an older woman who floated above his bed. To keep her away, he began shouting and was punching into and through the apparition. His fists landed against the wall, and woke up the guy sleeping in the next room.

"He was so afraid," Kurt said, "he said he was throwing punches at it and his fists were slamming into the wall. When we started to make fun of him, he got furious. He shouted it was real. He was sure he wasn't dreaming and the figure was right above his bed. This time he wasn't taking our dream theory as an excuse."

For days afterwards, the sightings were the main topic of conversation. But, the clock guy and the night visitor guy didn't want to discuss any of it. The other housemates eventually dropped the subject that the house might be haunted. But, Kurt said, each one of them was thinking there was more to the story than bad food causing indigestion and bad dreams.

Kurt's first encounter was in the form of an apparition that appeared at the foot of his bed.

"It was a tall, shadowlike figure," he recalled. "I woke up and lifted my head. At first I thought I was dreaming. Then, immediately, I was so scared. Even if I wanted to scream I couldn't. I was utterly breathless. It had on a black cloak, with a hood. I could just about make out its mouth and nose. After a few seconds, that seemed like a lot longer, I began blinking my eyes, trying to clear them, moving my head. Then, with what was a tremendous effort I was able to move my hand, and I smacked myself in the face, to see if I was really awake.

"I'm like really, really scared. I flipped on the light, but there was no one there. The heat was on high, but I noticed it was frigidly cold in my room. I could see my breath. I left the light on, got up and walked downstairs and slept on the couch on the first floor. The next morning, I told the guy in the second floor room, he was the one beating the wall, what happened. He believed me, because by now he was scared to death to live in that house."

Kurt told the others a few days later. Two laughed and the other, the clock guy, was quiet and didn't say anything.

"You see," Kurt said, recalling back to the time when everything that had happened was falling together, "it's almost a scary thing to admit. You're stuck there, so you deny it or dismiss it as long as you can. Some of them were saying I was bullshitting them to scare them even more than they were, or I was dreaming or I had an idea in my head and I manufactured it all. It's interesting to look back and see how people handle strange events that happen to them. They can live in denial for a long time, but they do it to survive."

Through all this time, which was about six months into their residency in the University Ghost House, Clyde the Dog continued to bark at unseen visitors; the sounds of phantom footsteps on the stairs and throughout the hall occurred frequently; and, while the guys were sitting in the kitchen, they would hear strange sounds coming from the dirt floored cellar—but no one ever went down to investigate. They all acted as if they heard nothing at all.

Now he's a believer and a secret room in the attic

It was, Kurt said, "the straight shooter accountant, the guy who didn't believe in ghosts and who wouldn't make up a story in a million years," who had the next sighting.

He would get up five times a night to go to the bathroom, which was down the hall from his second-floor room. One night, as he was heading for the toilet, he noticed a light on downstairs. That was unusual, since all five of the housemates made it a point to turn off the electricity in rooms not being used to save money.

"He told us he looked down the stairs, into the first floor," Kurt recalled, "and he saw a figure, floating across the living room. He said it was glowing. As it's going across the room, it pauses, turns its head, and looks up at him. He said it was an older woman, then she, or whatever it was, takes off and floats through the wall into the apartments next door.

"Now, he was obviously awake, since he was walking around. He ran up into the attic to get me and wanted me to go downstairs and look for it. I admit, I was afraid to go down. So he stayed up in the attic with me for the rest of the night."

Pausing, Kurt recalled what his friend said when he woke him up. "He said to me, 'Kurt, you remember the story about the woman floating in the second floor room? Well, I just saw her.' "

After this incident, Kurt said nearly everyone in the house was a believer or had an experience they wanted to forget. At this point, the previous nonbelievers were sharing notes and memories.

They said:

- The apparitions did not have feet and "sort of floated" around the room;
- A white glow surrounded the woman's whole body;
- Her face was old and you could see the wrinkles; and
- She wore a loose, flowing type of dress.

"For me it was especially scary," Kurt said. "I was all alone in the attic. There were three guys on the second floor and one in a room off the kitchen. But I was up there all alone—out of sight, out of mind. There also was this small door, set way in the back of my walk-in closet, that I could never get open. My father tried to help me open it when I moved in. He even used a crowbar, but it was painted shut, so we gave up. We put a small refrigerator in the main closet, in front of the sealed door. We just gave up on the back portion, but about this time I started to wonder what might be in there."

Just before leaving for a two-week Christmas vacation, Kurt said he pulled his refrigerator out into the room and opened its door to air it out. He gathered his bags of laundry and clothes and began to head out his bedroom door.

"Suddenly, I heard a creaking sound," he said. "I turned and my first thought was that the refrigerator door was moving. But it was fine. Then, it sounded like a 500-pound church door was swinging open on rusty hinges. I was freaked. I dropped my bags and ran to the first floor. I was in a panic. I grabbed one of the guys and pulled him back upstairs and told him to sit with me a few minutes on the steps outside my room.

"When there wasn't any sound, we went into my room and looked into the back of the closet. There was light coming from the small, sealed up door in the back corner. All the paint was cracked and chips were on the floor, like someone had pried it open.

"I said, 'We're out of here!' I shut the door and went home for two weeks. When I told people the stories about the place they said I was an idiot for staying there. My mother was upset. She wanted me to get a priest to go in and bless the place. Other people told me to get a room at Ho Jo's until the priest got the demons out.

"Then, when most people said I was nuts, I stopped telling the story. Half the people thought I was making it up anyway. But that didn't matter. I knew what happened. And that helped all of us, too. As soon as everybody thought we were nuts and crazy, we all agreed on what had happened and it pulled us together, because we were all in the same boat."

When Kurt returned from Christmas break, the five housemates went up into his room and the smallest guy, holding a flashlight, and with lots of moral support, crawled into the secret door.

Kurt said, "I remember him screaming out, 'You guys aren't going to believe this!' And carved into the molding around the inside of the door were the words, 'Karen died here.'

"At this point we didn't want to live there. Then we took flashlights and started looking around the house for any other messages. About two weeks later we found the words, 'Sarah is dead,' carved in the big closet in my room, in a rafter of the roof.

"You can imagine, by now we were all believers and we were totally freaked out. And no one would come up to my room, even the other guys who lived there stayed away from my attic. From that point on, no one would ever stay in the house alone. We would be sure someone else was there, friends, girlfriends."

Now she's a believer

Kurt's girlfriend, Shannon, like all the other guys' girls, thought that the football players were making up the ghost stories to scare them and see their reactions. She found out differently.

The two of them had fallen asleep in Kurt's room and, at exactly 3:08 a.m., he woke up and the room temperature was below freezing. Shannon, a cheerleader, was about one-fourth of Kurt's size. The minute his mind registered the coldness of the room, it immediately made a connection with the black-shrouded apparition he had seen months before at the foot of his bed.

Grabbing Shannon under one arm, he leapt out of bed. Both of them were screaming as he raced toward the door to carry her down the stairs.

"There was this awful feeling of dread in the room," Kurt said. "It was freezing, and it was like someone was there and going to kill us. I had a really bad feeling. And even though we didn't see anything, I know there was something evil in there that night."

The five guys lasted until the end of that year, then they found a smaller, "friendlier" place and turned the house back to the landlord. Kurt was moving out as two of the new group of student renters were going through the house, checking it out.

"I told them some of the stories I told you," Kurt said, shaking his head. "They thought I was giving them a load of bull, trying to scare them. But, at least they were warned. I don't think they rented the place, though. They said it was too expensive. But, it wasn't my problem anymore."

One last visit

A few months into the following school year, Kurt and his friends were hanging out at a Newark night spot, when a guy who lived in the University Ghost House came up and introduced himself.

He told Kurt that he and his friends had heard some of the stories about the place. Like Kurt's' group, the new residents didn't believe the stories, either, at first. Now, after a fair number of sleepless nights and unbelievable terrors, they were counting the weeks until they could end their lease.

He also mentioned that they had found a sealed up secret room behind one of the closets on the second floor—not in the attic where Kurt had tried to sleep.

Pumped up and high from a fair number of brewskis, four jocks and four of the new tenants headed back around midnight

Ghosts

to the Ghost House to see what was hidden behind the newly discovered secret door.

"It took four of us to pop it open," Kurt said, "and we were glad there were eight of us, but we were still scared to death. It had to be the beer that made me go back, because I never wanted to go in there again. I mean, the minute I entered the building I got the chills, and so did the other guys."

Behind the door, that they forced off its rusted hinges, was a narrow crawl space. Inside was an antique bathtub, full size with ball and claw feet. But there was no way to get it in or out of the opening. It was like the wall had been built there to seal it in.

"We aimed our flashlights in there," Kurt said, "and focused on the tub. It was streaked with rusty stains. They were running down the inside and edges. It really looked like dried old blood to me. They sealed it back up. One of the kids that lived there then told me that must be the portal to the other side, the place the spirits come in and out of. He said he can feel that that's the spot. I don't know, and I don't care. It's not my problem any more."

Kurt sat for a moment or two, then asked me what I thought of his story, if it was any good.

I assured him it was one of the best I'd heard in a while.

Then he asked me why it happened. He wanted to know what caused the sightings, the cold, the strange events. Was there a murder, a sudden death?

I had no answer.

"You know," he said, looking across the small coffee table, "before all this happened, I would laugh in somebody's face if they told me a story like this."

And now? I asked him.

"I'm completely serious, before all this happened to me, I would hear stories like this and think the people were nuts." Suddenly, all traces of humor left Kurt's face and his tone of voice became very steady, as if he wanted to emphasize what he was about to say. "Now," he added, "I believe in ghosts 100 percent. And everyone else who lived in that house with me believes in them, too."

A Short Ride from the Hancock House

So often, people are kind enough to give me, or try to share with me, ghost stories, that it's impossible to follow up with them all.

For at least three years, I had been doing programs in Salem County, New Jersey, and during a number of the programs Jill and her daughters would appear in the audience. And at the end of the campfire or talk, Jill would come up and remind me that I was going to call her about the ghost in her house.

Well, I guess she had heard enough promises, because in the spring of 2001, after two programs at the Hancock House on the close association between History and Haunts, Jill walked up to me and said, "Ed! I've got the girls waiting outside, and the motor's running. Let's go, and you can see my haunted house."

Having been ordered around by women since the nuns at St. Hedwig's Grade School directed me to kneel in the corner of the classroom several times a month, I knew better than to argue or offer an excuse.

Five minutes later we were heading southwest, down two-lane country roads surrounded by fields and wetlands, heading for Jill's former residence.

As I rode in Jill's Blazer, I thought about the historic site I had just left—Hancock's Bridge, New Jersey, a charming, but quite isolated, community in the middle of Salem County. If the village seems off the main thoroughfare today, I imagined how

Ghosts

out of the way it must have been during the days of the Revolutionary War. Apparently, however, the British were able to locate the site and massacre about three dozen members of the New Jersey Colonial Militia in historic Hancock House.

That event, which has prompted a moderate number of ghost tales, is well known in Salem County and beyond.

According to state park information fliers and old newspaper articles, William Hancock built the historic house in 1734 on land given to the Hancock family by William Penn in 1677.

During the Revolutionary War, a drawbridge at the site was a valuable transportation link and a small militia garrison was stationed at the settlement known as Hancock's Bridge.

During the winter of 1777-1778, while Gen. George Washington was camped at Valley Forge, Pennsylvania, Gen. Mad Anthony Wayne conducted foraging missions in the area of Wilmington, Delaware, and in Salem County, New Jersey.

The British also sent out foraging parties seeking food and supplies. In March of 1778, British soldiers, under Gen. Charles Mawhood, moved through Salem County and met with resistance from Salem County militia. Along the way, the British burned houses of American patriots, took what supplies they could and were intent on punishing the rebels who had provided assistance to Gen. Wayne and Gen. Washington.

On March 21, 1778, a British force of 300 men crept up Alloway Creek and surrounded the Hancock House, which is only a few hundred yards from the drawbridge. The invaders surprised the guards, entered the home, in which the militia was resting, and bayoneted more than two dozen locals inside. Approximately 20 men died immediately, others were to perish from serious wounds in the days and months to come. Among those killed in the raid was Judge William Hancock. Although, an American sympathizer, he also was an official of His Majesty's court and respected by both sides in the conflict.

Legends abound at sites where sudden death and tragedy are known to have occurred. In addition, with the passing years, decades and centuries, the stories become larger and the details embellished.

Are there ghosts in the Hancock House?

I have no idea. But, of course, there are rumors.

Some Salem County residents believe the ghost of Judge

Hancock, who the Redcoats bayoneted to death in his bed, still walks the halls and rooms of his historic home. One person told me she has seen the judge's ghost staring out from the second floor window.

One report states that the local militia retreated to the attic, where they were set upon and bayoneted and slain. For years, locals claim, the bloodstains remained imbedded in the floorboards.

Many "wish" for a good ghost story associated with the only Revolutionary War massacre in the state of New Jersey. As of yet, none has yet been found. But who knows when one will surface—ghosts have forever to make their presence known.

However, Jill was beginning to tell her personal ghost story. As she stopped her SUV at the edge of a dead-end street, she pointed to a two-story, gray frame house that obviously was vacant.

"There it is," she said, smiling. "And it hasn't been lived in since we left the place in 1991, an even 10 years ago."

Having done some research at the local library and the Salem County Historical Society, Jill said she was told the home dated back to the early 1800s and that, at different times, it had been a tavern, post office, pool hall and possibly even a speakeasy during Prohibition.

"It's had a lot of traffic in and out," Jill said, "so it would be hard to find out who the old woman ghost is. But she's for real. I've seen her, and so have my daughter, mother and my husband. But he won't admit it."

After moving into the home in the mid-1980s, Jill said she woke up one morning—when it was still very dark outside—and noticed an old lady sitting at the foot of her bed.

"I wasn't scared, not at first," Jill said, "because I thought it was a dream, but then I looked at the clock, and looked back, and she was still there. When I knew I wasn't dreaming, I started to freak out, and that's when she disappeared. In a flash."

Jill mentioned hearing footsteps, having doors that wouldn't stay closed and feeling cold spots and drafts. But she said she just shrugged all the odd things off, attributing the mini-spooky events to normal odd occurrences that came with living in a 200-year-old house.

Ghosts

When her daughter, Nancy, told her mother that an old lady was lying in the youngster's bed, Jill began to pay closer attention.

"We would hear whispering coming from different rooms, but you couldn't locate it or make out what they were saying. Then there was walking from the floors above and banging on the walls a lot. One day my mother saw the ghost but never told me right away.

"Then," Jill added, "a few weeks later my husband looked up and saw a figure walk by our room and he thought it was Nancy. So he followed her. But when he got to the bottom of the stairs, the figure turned and went into a room to the left. However, Nancy was playing with my mother on the floor of the living room."

When Bill asked his mother-in-law who had just walked through the room, the older lady said, "The ghost. Why don't you follow her and see where she went."

"Mother saw it," Jill said, "but she wasn't afraid of it. After a while, the sightings became more frequent, especially in Nancy's room. The ghost would appear in there about three times a week. Her school friends stopped coming over to play, and none of them would stay overnight in our house. No way. The word was out. We lived in the 'haunted house.' "

Jill recalled that some of her neighbors—both adults and children—mentioned that they had seen an older woman in a long, old-fashioned dress, sitting on the front porch.

While Jill had never seen that type of sighting, she wasn't going to dismiss the story and was inclined to believe it as a fact rather than a rumor.

The apparition was described as an older woman who sometimes wore a dark blue or gray cape. She looked real, Nancy said, "not misty or fuzzy. It looked like an actual person."

One night, in the middle of a hot summer evening, a series of strong banging sounds caused Jill's mother to shout out, "Check on the kids!" Jill ran up into her daughters' room and said she felt "like I walked into a freezer. It was cold as ice and scared me to death."

That incident was the turning event that drove the family from the house. Not too many days passed and they decided to give up the ghost and find another place to live.

A friend offered to help Jill pack up the house and move out. In the middle of a sunny afternoon, with boxes piled high and pieces of furniture and bed slats leaning against walls on the first floor, the ghost offered a farewell signal.

"My friend and I were sitting on the floor, resting," Jill said. "Suddenly, stuff started jumping out of the boxes and flying across the room. It was as if somebody had opened the lid and was throwing my stuff as hard as she could.

"My friend's eyes got as big as plates, and she got up and headed out the front door. She never came back. I moved everything else myself.

"When we left we never came back, ever," Jill said. "Oh, we'd ride by and say, 'There's our old haunted house!' But we've never stepped foot in there since that last day. Now, my mother said she'd go back, that she wasn't afraid, but she was the only one. I don't ever want to live there again. Neither do my kids or my husband."

Apparently, neither does anyone else.

The home, Jill told me, has been vacant since they left. She said they had heard through a friend that one tenant had moved in, but within two days he had moved out. It remains unoccupied.

As we started to head back toward Hancock's Bridge, Jill drove slowly in front of the vacant rental property. Nancy, who was in the back seat pointed to the building and said, "Hey, look, Mom! Isn't that your old lamp you left behind still up there in the back bedroom window?"

We all looked up at the stem of the shadeless lamp—alone in a second-floor window, offering proof that no one else had been able to exist in the haunted home that Jill and her family had left behind.

Haunted Barns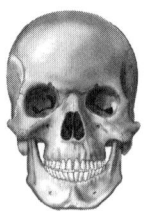

Barns have the ability to capture your eye, to make you pause and wonder. Drive along main roads and narrow roadways and you will see them, standing tall and impressive, sometimes weathered and neglected. If vacant, these large structures serve as reminders of long gone agricultural activity—of past times when man and wife, along with family members of three generations, lived off the land, directing plow and beast through open fields.

Those were hard-working, uncomplicated days, decades before sterile strip malls and cookie-cutter developments destroyed pleasant landscapes, and years before fast-food chain restaurants and oversized superstores put to death small family businesses and mom-and-pop storefronts.

Long gone are the good old days, before the arrival, like waves of locusts, of developers, land agents and speculators. But like them or hate them, you have to give them credit: these greed-obsessed land merchants made good on their promise—to deliver the benefits of "progress," which has consumed the Earth and left behind plastic, prefabricated temples of impersonal convenience.

But still a few scattered barns remain. Today, many of these silent sentinels are surrounded by new housing developments and overlook congestion and heavy machinery instead of mule teams and trappers at work. Their sagging beams hear the shrill sounds of traffic, instead of the soft songs of birds, and they watch helplessly as wildlife becomes transformed into road kill.

In some cases, these old rustic warehouses that sheltered dairy herds or dried tobacco leaves contain anything but pleasant memories. Certain ones hold memories of death, suicide and mass murder. The only problem is, we don't know which ones they are.

Final Farewell in the Barn

Along the Mason-Dixon Line, in a small town slightly west of the Delaware border and just into Maryland, Greg bought a big old house just off of the village's main street. He was only the second owner of the property—that included a frame house, outbuildings and a few barns that all had been built in the very early years of the 1900s.

Greg, who was in his 30s, and his wife, Marcy, raised their daughter there and spent considerable time restoring "this old house," as they called it. As a few years passed and the old Victorian began to take on a new, grand appearance, some of the family members of the previous owner would come by to talk and, even at times, lend a helping hand.

Marcy and Greg said they "loved the house to death," but after about 15 years had passed they decided to move into a smaller home on the Eastern Shore, overlooking the Chesapeake Bay.

The only problem was Greg was a collector.

"Collector is not the word," Marcy said, adding, "he is the biggest pack rat I know. He hoards and hides and never gets rid of anything, ever. In the beginning, I used to ask him if we should toss out something that was broken, but he always said, 'No! Hold onto it. I think we can use it for whatever!' So, eventually, I learned not to ask. I just threw out whatever I could when he wasn't around."

Greg would sort through the trash when he arrived at the dump—finding the items his wife had hidden in the bags and boxes, and he would bring back home about half of what he took to deposit.

"Our out buildings were pretty much filled to overflowing," Greg said, smiling at the memory.

This caused a problem when they put their home on the market, because it was going to take considerable time and effort to sort, empty, trash and transport the contents of several sheds and small barns, plus a large-size, two-story barn.

Fortunately, Marcy said, a friend purchased the property and agreed to allow Greg to take the time he needed cleaning out his shed and barn treasures.

Ghosts

"We took one building at a time," Greg said. "Even though my friend said we could take our time, we decided it would be best to get our stuff out and be done with sorting and cleaning as soon as possible. We held a number of yard sales and gave away a lot of what we didn't need."

"One night," Marcy said, "when Greg was in the largest barn, working all alone and cleaning out the last few things, he heard a scratching noise."

"I looked up," Greg said, jumping in to explain what happened, "and I noticed a nail puller that was hanging from a hook, right above me. It started swinging and swinging and swinging, back and forth. Now, no windows were open. There was no breeze at all, nothing that would explain the movement of this tool."

Greg said he stared at it and tried to figure out what was going on.

"I didn't think it might be a spirit right away," he said. "Then, all of a sudden, the thought flashed into my mind. I started talking to it as if it was something real or living. I was trying to figure out what was going on."

He began calling out the names of his deceased relatives and friends, like he was reciting a list from a family tree, trying to see if he could call out the right invisible being.

"I said, 'Mom, Dad, Grandpa, Uncle Jubal, Uncle Timmy, Aunt Grace, Aunt Netta, Cousin Lloyd, Billy and Stutters,' They were two of my older cousins who had gone on. I was trying to get a reaction."

"Finally," Marcy said, "it came to him that it was probably one of the former owners who had passed away and who was coming to say goodbye to him."

"I must of hit on which one it was," Greg said, " because I started talking to him. Thanked him for being good about the house, told them how much we had liked living there and assured them that the new residents were good friends and wonderful people, who were going to be just fine, would take care of things real good. I sat down and talked for a long time. It must have been almost a full hour. And the whole time, this tool kept swinging. It never stopped, until a few moments after I stopped talking."

Greg said he felt very satisfied after the chat with the swinging nail puller spirit.

"I figured that they knew we were leaving and that they had come to say goodbye," Greg said. "When it stopped swinging, I reached up, pulled it down, put it into my pocket and took it home with me. That was the end of that."

The nail puller sits on the front edge of a bookcase in Greg's new home. It doesn't hang from any nail or rafter, just rests flat on a shelf.

"I thought what happened was sort of interesting and a bit unusual," Greg said. "I know it's not horrifying. Maybe somebody would think it's just a little eerie, especially if it happened to you working all alone in a barn in the middle of the night. It's not the kind of material that great ghost stories are made from.

"But," he paused and added, "if that tool starts moving across the bookshelf or floating across the air, I'll be sure to call you back. 'Cause then I'd know we've got major developments for sure."

Hanging Beam in the Barn

In a dairy barn, located in Burlington County, New Jersey, a teenage boy was found hanging from a beam directly in the middle of the milking area.

Police ruled the death a suicide, although no note was found. Within a year, his depressed family sold the property and moved to rural Kentucky, where they started another dairy operation and tried to begin life again, hundreds of miles away from the tragedy.

The new owners, who knew about the young boy's death, tried to continue the dairy farming operation. However, their cows refused to enter the area of the barn where the boy had killed himself. No amount of brute force or kindly enticement could get the cows to stay in what had become known as "the haunted barn."

Eighteen months later, the farm and property were sold. Again, the new owners came up against what locals were now calling "the curse of the haunted barn." Apparently, the dead boy's spirit was still making his presence known to the animals that were being forced to live inside the building of death.

Eventually, the property was sold to an enterprising developer who didn't care what ill deed occurred at the site. To solve the problem and increase the size of his portfolio, he transformed the barn and surrounding meadow into an office complex. Unfortunately, the night watchman's desk and security cameras were located in the area where the boy's suicide had taken place more than 12 years earlier.

Employees who worked late into the evenings often complained about feeling cold drafts or passing through icy spots in the building. Others reported seeing the shadow of a quick moving dark figure traveling along the hallways, seemingly pressed up against the walls.

Initially, these employees thought they were seeing things and kept the sightings and feelings to themselves. But, after the security officers began telling their tales, work life at the "haunted barn" became anything but another boring day on the job.

It was late one evening, at about 11:30 p.m., when an older guard looked up from his fishing magazine and glanced, as he often did, at the set of four small security monitors stretched across the shelf located inches above his head.

His periodic checks usually took a few seconds, since he knew what to look for and was able to verify that everything was in place and undisturbed 99 percent of the time. On this occasion, less than a half-hour before midnight, his face froze when he saw the image of a dangling body. The neck was suspended by a noose at the end of a rope that led to a thick weathered barn beam. Automatically, as if directed by an invisible person at the controls, the camera zoomed in on the victim's face, revealing a bloated head with puffy lips, oversized eyes and a swollen tongue extending from its mouth.

The guard jumped back from the table, stared at the screen and pushed the intercom button on the desk phone. Although he was approaching a serious state of shock, he was conscious enough to realize that he needed a witness to verify the bizarre sighting. That was the only way he would be able to prove to everyone—including himself—that he was indeed not crazy.

When help arrived in the form of two younger, pistol-waving guards, the image of the dangling man was still on the screen.

At first, the two late arrivals thought the older man had been watching a movie and had turned the security camera to a commercial television or cable station. When they flicked the channels several times, all three men verified that the scene on the screen was real, at least as far as they could tell. Fumbling, they pushed in a recording tape to capture the images.

When they did so, the hanging man's image disappeared. Immediately, a view of the north parking lot, where the camera lens was mounted, replaced the swinging dead body.

The three men reported the incident to their supervisor, who told them to "forget it ever happened" if they wanted to keep their jobs.

They couldn't forget what they saw, but they did follow orders and avoided telling any of the workers.

But a story this good cannot go unspoken for long. Within a week, gossip about the "suicide in the haunted barn" was the talk of the complex—and not only within the barn building itself but in the offices and nearby warehouse, too.

Soon, cold spots and apparitions were reported at more than a half-dozen sites in the complex, and anyone who passed a slightly open door or an air conditioning vent claimed to have seen or felt the presence of "the ghost."

Two years after the first security camera sighting, an envelope was delivered in the mail to the complex manager and another identical package landed on the desk of the head of security. It contained copies of an old newspaper article about the original suicide, another story regarding the sale of the property to a local developer and a final piece on the dedication of the office complex.

No name was included with the report, and no one ever found out who had sent it. But the mystery of the "haunted barn" was solved—proof that you can never rely on a group of people to keep quiet about anything, especially when they suspect they might have the unfortunate luck to work in a haunted site.

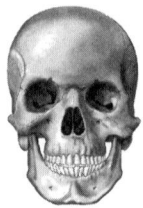

Only a Coincidence

Ever drive down the road and notice those old, abandoned cemeteries? They're in every county in every state and range from forgotten and ill kept three-acre plots surrounded by rusted chain link fences to those small, forgotten farm plots overrun with weeds in the middle of an open field.

Often these abandoned boneyards are marked with faded signs or rusted metal markers; others give no indication of the names given to these plots decades or centuries ago.

Whether you live on the Delmarva Peninsula, in New York's Southern Tier or on Florida's Panhandle, the story's the same—weathered gravestones, left behind without notice or care, are finding themselves surrounded by the ominous signs of progress. This advance of civilization comes in the form of housing developments, mobile home camps and suburban strip malls and shopping centers.

But what about the residents? Not the living newcomers moving in nearby—but the centuries-old tenants planted under the soil, the ones who thought they were going to rest happily ever after.

Should they be entitled to some say in what goes on around them?

And what role do they play in today's world?

Are these long-dead residents nothing more than eerie ornaments on the side of the road with no voice or purpose, or do they still have an important function?

At times, are they trying to tell us something, attract our attention?

Since they are not able to voice their displeasure at zoning board hearings or through letters to the editor, it's possible they have found other ways to make their presence and opinions known—and, more importantly, sometimes they can provide us with important, life-saving messages.

That's really what this strange story is all about.

It was after the Fort Delaware Ghost Tour, late one Friday night in the summer of 2000 when Charlotte and Mitch approached me at the Delaware City dock.

"We gotta good one for you," Mitch said, pointing to his wife, who he indicated had a ghost tale to tell.

Figuring I could get the story right then and there, they agreed to talk while sitting on a park bench in Old Battery Park, near a remnant of the lock from the original C & D Canal.

Nothing better, I said to the couple, than hearing a ghost story at 11 o'clock at night in the historic town's haunted park.

Charlotte smiled and Mitch snickered, and then I told them about the old man who fell into the lock and drowned—and that townsfolk had reported seeing his apparition, late on the summer evenings, floating back and forth along the old mule towpath only three feet from where we were sitting. That little fact set the mood and got their blood shivering and their lips moving.

Charlotte said her girlfriend lived on one of the main roads running north and south through Delmarva. It could be Maryland route 213 or U.S. 301, or Delaware 13 or 113 or old Route 1. It doesn't matter which road, except that it was a fairly wel traveled thoroughfare—the kind where passers-by tend to be in a rush to get to their destination and often overlook the scenery and landmarks that locals are aware of their entire lives—like a very old cemetery.

"My best friend, Heather," Charlotte said, "lived in a very small house with her husband and two children, right next to an old, abandoned cemetery. Now, things like that don't bother me, ghosts and graveyards and the like. I'm a chemist, so I don't believe in monsters and spirits and any of the other ghoulies they talk and write about. Me, I have to see it to believe it, and even then I'm skeptical. Working in a lab all day does that to

Ghosts

you. You think one thing, and 99.9 percent of the time the instruments prove you wrong. I've seen it happen time after time. So," she continued, taking a short breath, "I need to have a meter reading or certified ghostograph confirmation before I would accept any of these strange stories—even yours. No offense."

I assured her I was not bothered by her comment, had heard it hundreds of times.

"On the day this strange event occurred," Charlotte continued, "I was at Heather's place, getting my hair colored at her kitchen table. She's a hairdresser and does me favors so I don't have to go to the salon. She had two children, one on the floor beside us and the other was asleep in another room. I looked through the doorway that led into the living room. There was a little girl, about 7 or 8 years old, with long blonde hair."

Neither of Heather's children had long hair, and one was a boy. Also, the strange visitor was wearing a fancy Communion-style dress, but with no veil, and she had on white patent leather shoes and small white ankle socks.

"She was holding a small purse in her hands," Charlotte said, "and the girl stood there looking at me while I was frozen in place and looking back, straight into her bright blue eyes.

"Now, I began thinking that the fumes from the hair coloring conditioner were probably affecting me. So I closed my eyes, waited a few seconds, and looked up. But she was still there. Then I turned away again, this time praying that she would be gone by the time I looked back—but she was still there, as stiff as a statue."

One of Heather's kids, the older girl, was playing on the floor, in a corner of the kitchen where she couldn't see the Holy Communion girl. The boy, Richie, who was only 2, was asleep in his room down the hall."

Slowly and carefully, Charlotte said, she whispered to Heather that she should turn toward the other room to look at the young girl.

But after her friend, the homeowner, looked, she came back and said she didn't see a thing.

"I began to become agitated, because I could see the ghost or whatever it was plainly, and my friend—who lived in the house—was looking at me like I was crazy," Charlotte said. "Then Heather told me the house was almost brand new, too new to have any ghosts. She said that the first owners had moved out after living there for only about six months, and that was less than a year ago. While we were talking, I guess a bit too loudly, the Communion girl began to fade and disappeared, right in front of me. I have to admit, that made me feel very uncomfortable. I even got lightheaded."

When she paused, I reminded her that she told me at the beginning of our conversation that she did not believe in ghosts.

"I still don't, even after what happened next."

I waited for the nonbeliever to continue.

"For some unknown reason," Charlotte said, "the idea flashed into my head that Heather's boy, Richie, might be in trouble, in need of help. I asked where he was, and she said asleep down the hall. I told her to check in on him and she ran toward his room."

Heather's son had a serious case of asthma, and they always kept a radio monitor in his room, so that if he had trouble breathing the parents would be alerted. When the friend came back, she informed Charlotte that the monitor had been turned off and that Richie was gasping for air.

"Had she not checked on her son at that time," Charlotte said, "he might have choked to death and died. Heather thinks the Communion girl was an angel, sent to help alert us to Richie's danger. I don't know about that, but it certainly was good luck that she appeared when she did."

"Do you think the messenger was there to alert you, to try to tell you something?" I asked.

Charlotte said she didn't know, but the last part of her story added a new dimension, a final reason, perhaps, to the tale.

"A few months later," Charlotte said, "I got a call from Heather, who told me she was telling the story about the Communion girl to a neighbor who lived in a nearby farmhouse. The older lady told her about the young girl, about 8 years old, who died on her First Communion day from an asthma attack. And she's buried in the old abandoned cemetery at the end of the lane near Heather's house."

Heather believes the ghost of the young girl saved Richie's life. In fact, most people who have heard the story think that's a strong possibility. But Charlotte the scientist said she still doesn't believe in angels, ghosts, UFO aliens, friendly spirits or heavenly messengers—only coincidences.

Ghostly Guardian Angel

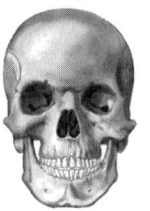

I had met Carrie during a storytelling program outside Philadelphia one cold November evening. During the presentation, I noticed that she seemed a bit more attentive than most of the other members of the audience, nodding approvingly to several of my descriptions of paranormal events and adding a few comments at appropriate intervals.

As I mingled with the audience afterwards, she said she wanted to share an unusual experience. The evening was still young, darkness was just beginning to fall, and we met about 30 minutes later in a corner of the hotel restaurant.

The King's Ransom had been built to resemble the interior of an Olde English pub. The builders had done a good job, as the intimate eating and drinking hole sported dark paneling, carved elf and gargoyle creatures peeking out from every corner and a crackling fire blazing from a large, walk-in-size stone hearth.

"My husband said I should tell you my story," Carrie said rapidly.

The statement came out like a gunshot, as if she needed to state that someone else had sent her to talk to the ghost man. Not many want to admit that they've demanded the meeting for their own sakes.

"He told me to tell you," she continued at machine gun speed, "that he's tired of hearing it from me. He said you could tell me if I was crazy, or if this thing has happened to anyone else. So what do you think?"

"Well," I said, smiling, "there's a very good chance I've heard something similar to your situation before—unless it's really off the chart, like you've got Bigfoot locked in your cellar or a Snallygaster caged in your yard. But, the problem is, you haven't told me what's going on."

Carrie laughed and relaxed. I guess realizing she was overly determined to explain why she didn't come on her own caused her to forget sharing her experience.

She was short, in her early 50s, with red hair. A gold chain around her neck was anchored with an irregular black stone.

"Interesting necklace," I said, nodding at the ornament.

"It was my grandmother's," she answered, lifting the stone from her body and holding it toward the center of the table. "It's nothing valuable, just a piece of rock from upstate, an odd sort of family heirloom. It's my good luck charm."

"You believe in luck?" I asked.

"Not really," she said, shaking her head. "You make your own luck. But I do believe in other forces, parallel dimensions, invisible visitors."

"Have you ever seen anything?" I asked, sensing we had already passed through the introductory phase and were moving swiftly into the essence of our reason for meeting.

"Yes. I believe I have," she said, calmly. "But, even more significant, in my mind, is that I have witnessed the results of others' experiences. And the timing of those events has convinced me that there are many more things operating around us that we can't see—but we can sense them, feel them and we can see their effects."

After only a brief pause, Carrie explained that she was referring to a series of incidents related to her maternal grandfather. "I believe that he was with me for many years after his death," she said matter-of-factly.

To understand her close feelings for this particular relative, Carrie said, I needed more background. She spoke of the late 1940s, when she was born in Philadelphia into a typical postwar, middle-class family. Her father, who had served with distinction in the Army during World War II, came home with millions of other men who were all looking for jobs, and ended up

Ghosts

with a job driving a truck for a large furniture company.

"Because the money was tight for my parents," Carrie said, my parents lived with my mother's parents until they could afford to buy their American dream—a house in the suburbs. I was born in 1946, and for the first five years of my life, we lived with my grandparents in a small West Philadelphia rowhouse.

"I was an only child, and my mother was as well." Carrie began to smile as she began to resurrect fond images of times long past. "We were both the apples of my grandfather's eye. I called my grandparents DeeDee and PopPop. As I grew up, PopPop was my tireless companion, and he played board games with me endlessly. We started with Chutes and Ladders and CandyLand, and eventually progressed to Clue, where he loved being Colonel Mustard."

Carrie told me how PopPop would read to her for hours, and he taught her how to do puzzles and play Fish. When summer arrived, she and her mother and grandmother would go to Ocean City, New Jersey, for the entire season.

"I looked forward to Friday nights," she said, getting a bit more excited and picking up the pace of her conversation, "when my dad and PopPop would arrive for the weekends. My grandfather would spend the weekends with me, walking for miles on the Ocean City boardwalk to take me to the 'kiddy rides' and buy me comic books and cinnamon buns at Simm's. We would take walks over to Chris's to watch the fishing boats come in, and he would buy his favorite rum buns! PopPop's favorite thing in the whole world was food, and he was much heavier than he should have been. Being the 1950s, no one was into healthy foods yet. So his diet was pretty much atrocious. He was an eighth-generation Pennsylvania Dutchman and carbohydrates ruled his days."

Suddenly, Carrie paused, took a sip of her drink, and lifted her face—to keep a budding tear from falling from her eye. "PopPop died when I was only 16 years old," she said, her pace a bit slower. "He was not yet 70, and that was such a shame. It happened a good 30 years before my grandmother died.

"So here's where we get to the interesting part," she added quickly. "A few nights after his death, something woke me up in the middle of the night, and I was sure that I saw PopPop standing in the dormer alcove of my bedroom. I screamed for my mother, and I remember her saying that seeing my grandfather should never scare me. She told me that I should be happy that he was around to protect me. But she did not believe that it was anything more than my dreaming."

Years passed without too much activity, but Carrie said she would never forget the night when she saw what she still believes was probably PopPop's apparition.

Carrie married her high school sweetheart in the late 1960s. Shortly before his death, her grandfather had met the groom.

"I was very saddened that he was not alive for my wedding, or for the birth in the following years of my first two children," Carrie said. "It was when my daughter, Lane, was about 15 months old that things started to happen. These unusual events, plus my own feelings and belief in the hereafter, caused me to realize that PopPop was not far away."

Carrie's first husband, Bill, was in the Army. When Lane was only three months old, he was sent to Vietnam. Carrie moved into her parents' home with her daughter for the duration of Bill's tour of duty.

"When Lane got to the point of talking," Carrie said, "I would hear her, usually at night, laughing and talking when she should have been asleep. When I went into the room to check on her, I would discover her reacting to what appeared to be someone tickling her. She would not be looking at me, but to the spot next to me, as though someone were standing next to me at her crib and talking to her.

"She would respond to this invisible 'person' by shaking her head and saying things like 'Yes' and 'No.' This happened a few times before I asked her who she was talking to, and she pointed to the space next to me and said, 'The big man!'"

Carrie said she and her mother knew immediately who the big man was. PopPop had returned. But Carrie said they didn't want to put any ideas into the little girl's mind, so they didn't say anything about the incident. They waited until the next time Lane indicated that the invisible visitor was present.

"One morning," Carrie recalled, "we were sitting at the table in the dining room and Lane's eyes lit up. Suddenly, she pointed to the bottom step of the nearby stairs and said, 'There he is. The big man!' My mother and I saw nothing, but I asked her what the big man said to her. She told me that he said he loved her and wanted her to be good to me."

Carrie's mother went into her bedroom and brought out some photographs. Slowly, they began going through them, making sure that Lane could see them as they fell onto the living room table. They were waiting—hoping actually—that the child would see someone she recognized.

"Before long," Carrie said, "my little daughter pointed to one picture of PopPop and said, 'That's my big man!' Prior to that," Carrie said, looking at me from across the table, "I am sure that we had never shown her a picture of PopPop, and there was none framed or on display in my mother's house. That's when I was sure, without a doubt, that PopPop was there."

When Lane grew older and began to speak more, she didn't talk about PopPop much, and his visits became less frequent. A year and a half after Bill returned home from Vietnam, a second child, Jeremy, was born.

"When he was about a month old," Carrie said, "the unusual activity started again. But this time, it was almost constant. I always felt my grandfather's presence. It was amazing, especially when Jeremy began to exhibit the same signs that Lane had, of being tickled and responding to someone who was in the room but unseen."

Tragedy struck when Jeremy was 13 months old. He was diagnosed with cancer, and he only survived until the age of three.

"There was a tremendous amount of activity while my son was alive," Carrie said. "And I always found a comfort in knowing that PopPop was nearby and that Jeremy was not alone during all of those hospital stays. But after his death, the activity stopped. I am convinced that PopPop was with us to comfort us before and after Jeremy's death."

Several years later, when Carrie was planning her wedding to her second husband, she had a dream the night before the formal ceremony.

"I saw my grandfather sitting in a pew with my grandmother, who had died a year before the wedding," she said, "and they were holding Jeremy, who was seated on PopPop's lap. They were all smiling and blowing kisses. I knew then that they were happy about my upcoming wedding, even if they had never thought in their wildest dreams that such a thing would happen.

I also knew that Jeremy was safe, and that he was happy with his great-grandparents."

Carrie said she tries to keep her children and her grandchildren aware of Jeremy's spirit. She refers to him as the "older brother that they never knew" and tells them that Jeremy is their guardian angel, and that he will always be there to comfort them.

Carrie is not hesitant to let anyone know that she also believes in guardian angels—and she said that they do their job very well.

"During my pregnancy was the one time I knew PopPop was in evidence," she said. "I was driving to work on the West River Drive in Philadelphia, and I was in the right-hand lane, next to a wall. I was approaching a bend in the road. But before I got to the turn, I distinctly heard PopPop's voice say 'Blowout!'

"By instinct, I moved to the left-hand lane. Thank God, there was no one there! And after I came around the bend, in the lane where I had just been, was a car, stopped with a blown-out tire. If I hadn't moved to the other lane, I would have surely hit the car and it would not have been a minor accident."

We sat for several silent seconds, letting Carrie decide if there was more to share.

"So that's my story," she said, a little shyly. "I probably went on and on, and maybe it's not as interesting as most of yours."

I held up my hand, asked her to stop apologizing. "It was fine," I said. "You loved your grandfather and son very much. I can tell."

"I still love them," she said, mildly correcting me. "I hope I have been able to convey how important it was to me to have had my grandfather's influence in my life, both in his lifetime and afterwards."

I told her that message was very clear.

"We've never heard or seen any activity from PopPop again, but I am convinced his job is done. My parents have now joined them and I am sure Jeremy is very well protected. And that makes me feel very good."

We talked a few moments more, and I told Carrie that what she had told me, about her children seeing an invisible being, was a common occurrence.

"Pets and small children are among the most innocent of

Ghosts

beings," I said. "Many people believe they are lucky enough to still have the essence of the gift—to see into the other side—that most of us lose as we grow older."

Ghosts are much more than horrifying creatures lurking in the shadows of the night. Sometimes, they're familiar beings who still care, who come back to help, to reassure us that things will be better when we all meet again on the other side.

Since so much of my time is spent searching for the dark side of the afterlife, talking to Carrie helped me remember that there's a bright side waiting for us, too.

House Ghost

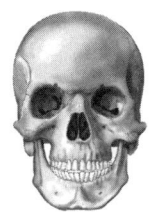

Victoria was an older woman who was born in Lewes in the 1930s and lived in the watertown her entire life. She had a story to tell and said so in no uncertain words.

"I came here to see you," she said, sitting across the table in Lewes' Dockside Gift Shop, overlooking the old canal. "I want to tell you a good ghost story that happened here in Lewes. And I know it's true, 'cause it happened to my family."

I was all ears. Mary Perez, the shop owner, moved over and said she was interested in hearing the tale, too, as did two regular customers—Robbie and Bob from Smyrna—who edged a bit closer to hear what Victoria had to say.

"My mother had a baby, in 1929, and they lived right here in Lewes," Victoria said. "My father worked at the powerhouse, and my mother would wait up for him to get home from work. She would read by the kerosene lamp. They didn't have no electric or water. One night, my mother said she felt like somebody was watching her, and she thought that Daddy had slipped on in unannounced. So she turned and there was an old lady in a black cape with a hood over her head, standing in the living room looking down on my mother.

"She froze and stared back at the creature, and finally said, 'What do you want?' But she got no reply. Then she got up, picked up the baby and went next door to the neighbors. My mother told the lady next door, 'There was something in that house that doesn't belong there.' "

Later, Victoria said, her mother would hear crying coming from the baby's room, but when she went in her child was fast

Ghosts

asleep and not making a sound.

Appearances by the silent apparition and the sound of a phantom baby's cries went on for years. The sightings were so common that they didn't bother Victoria's mother after a while, but she found the crying quite annoying.

"My mother," Victoria recalled, "she used to say, 'I don't mind that old lady standing in back of me, 'cause at least she's quiet.'"

Eventually, someone told the family that a tragic accident was the cause of their problems. Years before, on the second floor of that home, a mother picked up her crying baby. But while walking it, she accidentally dropped it down the stairs and it died. Those two ghosts were probably the ones who haunted the old house.

"The crying and walking and visions went on for years," Victoria said.

The baby was just a crier, but the adult ghost had a few tricks that it liked to play. One of its habits was lowering the side slats of Victoria's baby's crib. She said you could hear the sounds of the latch disengaging and the screech of the wooden section of slats being lowered.

"One night my uncles were over and they heard the sounds," Victoria said. "My mother told them it was just the old lady playing with the crib. Of course, they didn't believe her, thought she was nuts when she added that it was the normal activities of our house ghost."

One brother announced he was going to come back with his shotgun filled with rock salt, and he returned with a loaded gun and his black Labrador retriever named Ralph.

"That dog was wonderful with us," Victoria said, recalling her days as a young girl. "But, to tell you the truth, to everybody else, it was the meanest dog on the beach. Well, it was wintertime, and my uncle sat down in the corner of the baby's room, with Ralph by his side, and waited for the railing to move.

"We're all in bed, but we heard what happened the next day. Seems Ralph's ears went up, all of the sudden like, and my uncle went on alert. Then, for the first time in its life, Ralph put its tail between its legs and headed out through the door and down the steps. Then, it was clawing like crazy to get out the front door. My uncle was running right behind, scared to death, 'cause he heard the latch of the crib but there was nothing to see in the room.

"For years it just went on and on like that, strange things. My mother and father put up with the ghost, because that's where they lived. They just had to deal with it."

One year, a quarantine in the town caused Victoria's grandmother to be confined to the old house for a period of time.

"Before my grandmother went off to sleep," Victoria recalled, "my father was teasing her, saying, 'The old ghost is gonna come to see ya tonight. You wait an' see. She'll be up there around midnight.'

"Well, my grandmother had a habit of sleeping with her feet hanging out off the side of the bed. The next morning, she reported that the ghost had made an appearance. She said to us, 'That ghost came right up the steps and into my room. I wanted to bring my feet in so bad, but I couldn't move a muscle. Then, that ghost looked right at me and disappeared, went down under my bed. I tell ya this,' my grandmother said, 'that ghost don't want us here.' "

Soon afterwards, Victoria's family bought a lot near the beach and built a new house. Her grandmother was pleased that they left the haunted house in town.

"New people moved into the old house," Victoria said, "but they moved out quickly. They might last one night or two, and they were out of there. As I recall, it stayed vacant until it burned down one night.

"But," Victoria said, "it is true. They come back and they are back. I don't know if they don't believe they're dead or they don't want to be. The day after my husband died, I saw his favorite rocker in the front room started rocking on its own.

"I told him, 'John, you're dead! Leave me alone. Don't do this to me!' Then I took that old rocker that was still in real fine condition to the dump."

Short Sightings

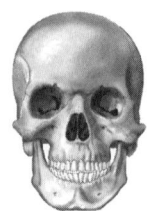

Still at Work

Ted works security at an old military base on the East Coast. The fort was active during World Wars I and II as a coastal defense installation. During the early half of the 20th century, the place was hopping with thousands of soldiers and civilian defense contractors. There also were hundreds of administrative personnel keeping records and documents up to date in scores of busy offices.

Driving his vehicle through the old post's narrow lanes is the easy part of Ted's job. Walking through deserted buildings is a bit more bothersome, especially when things happen that shouldn't, he said.

"I swear I've seen ghostly figures, apparitions," Ted said. "This place has a lot of history, saw plenty of action, and I guess a few of the guys who were here decided to stay. As I drive around, especially at night and in late afternoon when the sun is going down, I'll see movement, like floating figures, out of the corner of my eye. Sometimes they'll wait for me to turn and look for them. Then they'll disappear before I can get a good look at them. But I know they're there."

Solitary, midnight visits to the underground morgue are particularly unnerving.

"That can be a real creepout," Ted said. "It's in the old medical center. Closed up now, it's still there, down in the basement. There's one examination table and the refrigeration unit still works. I guess they figure it might be needed again one day. Sometimes, I'll turn the light on and it will go off on its own. Or I'll shut it off and come back later and it will be back on.

"That shouldn't happen. No one else is here except me during the graveyard shift. I'll be going down the hallway and feel an icy chill, like I walked through a freezer. Or I'll see a key, attached to a chain along the wall, swinging on its own. But there's no breeze or draft to make it move."

Shrugging his shoulders, Ted smiled, then added, "I just think to myself: Leave me alone. I'll be outta here in a minute. And then I get back upstairs and its over—for the time being. I don't really like walkin' the morgue."

Elevators have a way of traveling on their own at the old fort.

"They'll stop at a floor. The doors will open, and they'll be empty," Ted said. "I mean, no one's there. Sometimes I'll even hear voices, male voices mostly, coming from inside the elevator, but when I get closer to make out what they're saying, the voices stop.

"But there's been lots of death here. Who knows what kind of operations they did in the old medical building. They took the bodies on those elevators down to the morgue. I guess some of those death spirits have stayed around."

One in particular seems to be present in a certain old transportation administrative office.

"That's the ghost typist," Tom said. "All of the security guards agree there's something up there. No question. The story is that many years ago, a typist used to work late. One Friday afternoon she decided to get some work done and stayed late. Apparently, she died while typing at her desk. But because she lived alone, and the fort offices were closed for the weekend, no one discovered her until Monday morning.

"They say she was sitting upright, with her fingers over the keys. I don't know if that part of the story is true, but I can tell you I've heard the typing, and so have other guys. And when you open the door to the room, there's no one inside—and no typewriter either. It's used for overflow storage now, but still the typing continues from time to time. It's not supposed to happen, but it does."

Haunted Farms

Flying Farm Objects

An old farm field in Talbot County, Maryland, is believed to be haunted. A number of workers complained that rocks, vegetables and sticks were being thrown at them during the workday. However, there was no one else nearby, and they could never figure out the source of the disturbances.

Farm Prank Gone Bad

On an isolated homestead on the Eastern Shore, there's the story of a ghost that roamed the roadside scaring passing wagonloads carrying workers and residents.

One evening, two friends decided to take advantage of the legend and frighten the locals. One of the men covered himself in a white sheet, and planned to jump out and terrorize anyone who came along the road. Unfortunately, one nervous resident who saw the ghostly figure was so alarmed that he shot at the ghost and killed the young man imitating a phantom beneath the white flowing sheet.

Of course, his restless spirit continues to appear, warning others not to imitate a spirit lest you may become one yourself.

Fortune in the Field?

The last farm-related tale involves a young boy who told his family members that he had seen an old man near the ancestral graveplot, located beside the old frame farmhouse. Since no one else in the family saw the spirit, they all made fun of the boy and sent him on his way.

After several sightings, one night the boy left his small bedchamber and followed the phantom—who was dressed in old-fashioned clothing and was shrouded by a thick white mist—into the woods. There, the apparition pointed to the ground and directed the young boy to dig.

Following the ghost's silent instructions, the boy carved a deep hole into the ground and discovered a strongbox filled with gold.

Whether or not he shared his good fortune with his skeptical family members will never be known.

Ed Okonowicz

Ghost in Aisle 9

Northeast of Baltimore on U.S. Route 40, a lady in black lace is said to haunt an old supermarket.

"Everybody talks about the ghost," Harold said. A retired vegetable stocker and meat cutter, he explained that he had worked for many years at the store, and he stressed that he knew what he was talking about.

Harold guided me over to a corner of Washington Street Books and Antiques Shop in Harve de Grace and filled me in on the rest of the story.

"Since forever she's been there," he said. " Now, I never saw her, but other people say they have, and more than just a few. But I think I heard her once."

One night while working in the first-floor butchery, Harold recalled that he heard the sounds of heavy footsteps, like a person running. The sounds were coming from above, in the ceiling over his head.

"I looked up, surprised," he said, " 'cause nobody else was upstairs that night. I ran up there and looked around—saw nothing at all. When I told the guys the next day, they all said it was just 'the ghost.' That's what everybody called her. She didn't have a name as far as I knew."

One worker reported seeing the figure in black lace running down the aisles.

"That one guy who saw it," Harold recalled, "he said he chased her up and down the aisles and across the store. Never caught her, though, and she just disappeared. Another guy was in a room, doing some paperwork and the light switch on the wall moved and shut the light off. The guy told me he went over and flipped the switch up, turning the light back on. Then it happened again. So he got up and turned the light on again.

"When the light went off after that, the fella yelled out, 'All right! If you want to keep the light off, keep it off. It don't bother me.' And he left the room and that was it. Everybody figured that it was the ghost, going at it again."

Harold has no idea who the ghost may be or why the lady in black lace haunts the supermarket. All he knows is that she is there.

"Everybody talks about it, like it's a fact," he said. "They've all accepted her, and that's it."

Ghosts

Pig Woman Legends

Next to the Legend of Screaming Polly (I have yet to unearth that complete story and welcome any further information), the North East, Maryland, Pig Woman is mentioned quite often to me during talks and book signings.

The Legend of the Pig Woman has taken on many versions, and here are the three that I have heard frequently.

Fire on the Farm

Two young girls were walking down the road and noticed a fire blazing in an old farmhouse. As they stood back and watched the flames consume the residence, they saw an old woman fall from the second floor window and land on the ground.

The girls raced forward to help the burning woman, who was screaming at the top of her voice. As they approached and got within arm's reach of the smoldering flesh, the stench caused each girl to cover her nose and mouth. Suddenly, the old woman rolled over and jumped to her feet.

With smoke surrounding her charred body, she faced the schoolgirls, who immediately turned and ran when they saw the old lady's disfigured face, which they described as "a burnt piece of meat that looked like the face of an ugly pig."

From that day on, the story of "Pig Woman" has been told. In particular, the unsightly monster is said to live in the woods and riverbanks outside North East and appear late in the evenings, crossing backroads, on her way to find food to steal or an unattended young child to scare to death and take home and eat for dinner.

Meet Her at the Wooden Bridge

Some say if you pass over an old wooden bridge on a side road in the forests south of North East, your car will stop unexpectedly. But don't fear. You aren't alone.

Within moments, you will hear scratching on the fenders, trunk, roof and hood. When you regain control of your senses and push aside the overwhelming sense of sudden fear, you will see the distorted face of Pig Woman, pressed against your side window or front windshield, as her hands bang against the car demanding entry.

Those who leave the car seeking help are never seen again and apparently become her victims.

But those who are brave enough to stay in the car are better off and usually escape the wrath of the North East monster. Eventually, the vehicle's engine will turn over. When this happens, the driver will most likely speed away. But when he or she returns to the safety of the home driveway, the poor shaken driver will notice distinct pig hoofprints all over the body of the car.

Anyone who has encountered the Pig Woman refuses to drive that road again, whether alone or accompanied, and not in the day nor in the evening.

She Lives Near the Dump

This last version of the Pig Woman was shared with me by a former folklife teacher at North East, Maryland, High School.

In the 1960s, this source was involved in teaching folklore to students and, as a result of their research and writings, the class discussed and studied the Legend of the Pig Woman.

Apparently, the Pig Woman was more likely a resident of the Rising Sun, Maryland, area in northern Cecil County, located near the Pennsylvania state line.

Teenagers in those days were in the habit of parking late at night in an area near the Rising Sun dump site. An old woman, who had a contorted figure and a pig-like head, complete with a snout of a nose, would come out of the woods and beat on the windows of the teenagers' cars.

As the scared couples drove off in the darkness, they could see the ominous figure of the Pig Woman, waving her arms and shouting in the distance.

Ghosts in the Cotton Field

It was a beautiful day in Churchville, Georgia. The birds were chirping and the sun was shining bright. Staci Lynn Montgomery sat on the front porch of her new house, the third in the last two months, and gazed at the parcel in front of her. She wondered if it was a rule to give fruit baskets to new neighbors; after all, she had lived in 13 of the 50 states of America, and her family hadn't run out of fruit yet.

Staci was what some would call a military brat. Since her father was in the service, moving was old hat to Staci. But because of the constant moving, Staci was unable to make lasting friends, and as a result, she was a rather lonely child. She found refuge in reading, drawing and babysitting. After all, no matter where her father moved her next, there would always be paper, pencils, books and children waiting there for her attention.

This time the new destination was Churchville, Georgia. For Staci it was just another stop along the way. It was a tiny, quiet town, surrounded by large farms and even larger farm houses. Each building looked alike—tall and white with black shutters, and each had a long stone driveway.

For a girl of 15, the town seemed to offer nothing, until one night Staci overheard a conversation between her parents and a new neighbor. From what she had gathered, Churchville was home to several cotton plantations before and during the Civil War. Many of the huge houses that sat on these plantations had been remodeled and were occupied. However, according to the neighbor, people weren't the only modern-day residents. Some believed many of the occupants were ghosts.

Immediately, Staci took a liking to her new home, for mysteries were her specialty. But, she decided to put this little mystery on the back-burner, because the very next day she found a small classified ad in the town newspaper seeking a babysitter. And working for some extra spending money seemed like a more realistic job than hunting for ghosts.

The advertisement read:

"Great kids, beautiful house, in search of a babysitter. 1 boy/1girl ages 5/3 years. Three nights a week, 6-9 p.m....$6/hour! Call Daniella @ 676-1189."

Staci responded to the ad the next day, and was hired immediately. She wondered why someone had not already been chosen for the job. But she wasn't complaining, because this job sounded great, and Daniella, the mother, had asked Staci to start working the very next evening.

On her first day of work Staci rode her bicycle down to the house. Like all the other homes in town, it was a huge white farmhouse, with tall bright columns on the porch, black shutters and a long stone driveway, with a turnaround at the top. She parked her bike and Daniella invited her inside.

The family dog was lying under the kitchen table, whimpering non-stop.

The kids, Tyler and Ginger, were in the living room watching television and eating peanut butter and jelly—their evening snack. Daniella left Staci simple instructions: Have the kids in bed by 8 p.m., give Ginger a bath before putting her to bed, and make sure that Tyler brushes his teeth.

The mother grabbed her purse, kissed the kids goodbye, and headed for the door, with one final message . . . "Oh, and Staci, just one more thing. Ginger sometimes has trouble getting to sleep because she is afraid of ghosts. If you just reassure her that

Ghosts

there is no such thing, and read her a little story, she should be fine. Thanks! Gotta run," and she was gone.

Staci closed the door, went to the kitchen and cleaned-up the room a bit. Being in a strange house, she took some time to get adjusted. But she couldn't stay focused on cleaning because the dog was still lying under the kitchen table whimpering. Irritated by the mutt, she finished the dishes as quickly as she could.

Leaving Tyler to watch television, she carried Ginger upstairs to her room to get the little girl ready for her bath. All of a sudden, Ginger started fussing in baby-talk. She was smart for her age, but some of her sounds were still a little off...usually the pronunciation of her R's and W's.

"I no wanna go in woom. No go in woom, NO GO IN WOOM!," Ginger cried.

Staci, baffled by the child's agitation and growing outburst, calmed her down and asked what was the matter.

"No go in woom, pease Staci, no go in woom," Ginger cried, this time a little quieter. She pushed her way out of Staci's arms and ran off towards the bathroom. Letting her go, Staci went into the bedroom to get the child's night clothes.

She opened the bedroom door to find that the good-sized chamber was unusually cold. With the help of a glow from a small decorated night-light, Staci could make out the shape of a lamp sitting on the child's nightstand. As she went to turn it on, she noticed that it was sitting beside a rocking chair, which for some reason was rocking.

Staci figured that Daniella had been sitting in it before she left, and that it hadn't stopped moving yet. From what Staci could see in the dim light, the child's room was nicely decorated, with a gorgeous bay window, bright pink curtains and a beautiful bedspread featuring a rose design. Staci wondered what Ginger detested about her wonderful room.

As Staci reached for the light, the bay window suddenly blew wide open with a bang. Cold, crisp night air blew in, making the hairs on the back of her neck stand straight. She went to the window, trying to avoid getting tangled in the pink curtains which were twisting and twirling as though they were caught in a whirlwind. Quickly she shut and locked the window. Then, quivering, she found Ginger's night clothes as fast as she could, ran from the room and slammed the door shut behind her.

The dog, which had at some point moved from under the table, followed close at Staci's heels...whimpering.

Spooked, Staci hurried to give Ginger a bath and get her ready for bed. Since Tyler brushed his teeth, she decided to tuck him in first. After all, Ginger seemed like she was going to have a little trouble getting to bed.

After leaving Tyler's room, Ginger and Staci made their way down the hall to the little girl's room. This time Ginger was hesitant, tugging harder on Staci's hand as they approached closer to the bedroom door, but she remained quiet and did not fuss.

With the dog close by Ginger's side, Staci pushed opened the door and the dog and the child hopped straight into bed. Staci gave her a kiss on the cheek, tucked the covers under her chin, and turned to leave.

But she didn't get far before Ginger started chanting, "Sto-wie! Sto-wie! Sto-wie!"

Staci went to the bookshelf and grabbed the first book she could find—Cinderella. She climbed onto the tiny space left toward the foot of the bed and opened the book. She started to read when all of a sudden Ginger says, "You no wead like Mista James weads."

"What Ginger?" Staci asked.

"You no wead like Mista James weads."

"Who is Mister James?"

"He's da black man. He comes in my woom thwew the window and weads me stowies."

"Does he read you Cinderella?"

"Mr. James reads me all kinds of stowies."

"Is he here tonight Ginger?" Staci asked, slowly scanning the room with her eyes, which were getting a bit wider as she wondered what she might see.

"No silly, cause you closed da window," the child replied with a knowing grin.

"Oh," Staci said, and began to read the book. She continued until she reached the part about the wicked stepsisters. At that point, Ginger exclaimed, "They aw like Mista Potta."

"Who is Mr. Potter, Ginger?" Staci asked, not sure that she wanted to know the answer.

Ghosts

"He is da white man who sits in the wocking chair. Mista James no like Mista Potta. And I no like Mista Potta either. He's scawy."

Now Staci was spooked. First it was the dog who wouldn't stop whimpering. Then Ginger absolutely refused to go in her room. The locked window had somehow mysteriously blown open, and now Ginger had concocted some strange story about ghosts. Ghosts that not only existed, but ghosts who came through windows, read her stories and sat in rocking chairs.

Staci continued with Cinderella until Ginger fell asleep, then the babysitter replaced the book on the shelf and left that room as fast as she could.

During the next three evenings Staci baby-sat for Ginger and Tyler, unusual things happened much like they did that first night. Because of this, Staci had made it a point to keep the house well lit. On the fifth night, however, even the illumination of a house full of lights didn't help. Ginger absolutely refused to go in her room after her bath, so Staci decided to take her downstairs to watch TV, hoping that the little girl would fall asleep.

As cartoons ran across the screen, the dog, standing at the foot of the steps, started to bark loudly. Staci got up in an attempt to quiet him, and as she bent down to pet him, he bared his teeth and started to growl at her. Then, almost simultaneously, the television and living room lights started to flash off and on, off and on!

Ginger, afraid of the dark, started to shriek at the top of her lungs. Staci ran to the couch to comfort the poor child and explain that it was just a little power outage. But Staci knew there wasn't anything wrong with the power, because the lights in the kitchen and pantry were still on. She just didn't want the child to know that she, her protector, also was scared.

Staci's fear did not get a chance to subside, for Tyler ran from his room calling out, "STACI! STACI! There's a man in my room! He's in old clothes and walking all around."

"See Staci, I told you them awe ghosts," Ginger said, forcing the words out along with her tears.

"Guys, let's calm down, okay?" Staci said, trying to take control. "There are no such things as ghosts!"

"But Staci, there are ghosts in our house, Mommy and

Daddy talk about it all the time," Tyler admitted calmly.

Just then, all the lights in the house went off. Ginger again started to scream. Abruptly, the windows in the kitchen, which could be seen from the living room, blew open, the curtains swaying furiously in the cold night air. Staci, her head spinning and heart pounding, grabbed the two children sitting next to her, and pulled them close. Frozen in terror, the three of them huddled behind the couch until 9 p.m. when Daniella finally came home.

The lights had come back on right before Daniella's car turned into the driveway. When the children saw their mother, their fears diminished. They both went back to watching TV, as Daniella and Staci walked into the kitchen.

Staci told the owner about the spooky things that had been happening, and about the crazy stories Ginger had told her.

Daniella had a funny look on her face and sat down at the table with Staci. She said that Ginger had told her the same stories. She said that Daniella and her husband had purchased the house from an old widow, who found it too large to maintain. The woman had never mentioned anything about the house being haunted. The old owner, basically, Daniella said, had taken their money and run. Daniella said she first thought that their new house was haunted when they had hired some painters to redo the outside of the farmhouse.

In the middle of the night, one of their neighbors at the farm had called them while they were still living at their old apartment. She asked Daniella if the painters were working overtime. After Daniella told the caller no, the woman informed her that she had seen two tired looking black men in overalls wandering around the house. Daniella asked her to look back out the window to see what they were doing.

When the caller returned on the line, she told Daniella the two men were walking away from the house out into the fields. Both women figured the men were just trespassers and decided not to worry.

However, when Daniella and her husband went to see their house the next day, they discovered that the owner of the painting company was furious with them.

"Why did you people hire other painters? Is there something wrong with my crew?" the contractor asked, clearly upset.

Ghosts

"We didn't hire anyone else," Daniella replied.

"Then who are those two painters around back? They don't work for me!"

As the painter and the couple walked around back to confront the men, they noticed two, somewhat translucent figures dressed in overalls, walking away from the house out into the fields. Daniella realized that these must be the men that her neighbor had reported seeing the night before. She told her husband what she knew, and the two painters were not seen again after that.

Now Staci was convinced that the house really was haunted, and she informed Daniella that this was the last time she would be babysitting for Tyler and Ginger. Daniella, who had been very satisfied with Staci's reliability, tried to get the young lady to stay on, but Staci had made up her mind. She had enough nights in the haunted house. She called her mom to come get her. There was no way she was riding her bike home that night.

As the weeks passed and Staci had gotten over her initial fears of the haunted babysitting job, she became intrigued with the history of the plantation. On a trip to the library, she decided to dig up some information on former occupants of the haunted house.

According to an old reference book about the history of Churchville, Mr. Potter had been a wealthy cotton plantation owner who had owned many slaves. Like a number of slave owners in the past, he was a mean and difficult man. In addition to field work, his slaves performed work around the grounds, including the painting of the large, and very tall, plantation home.

Reading on, Staci discovered that Mr. James was a self-educated slave who had been owned by Mr. Potter. Because of his knowledge and leadership among his fellow slaves, Mr. James was considered a constant threat by Mr. Potter. The plantation owner also was afraid that Mr. James would lead an attack against him.

The owner decided that the best way to break Mr. James' power and resistance was to sell off the educated slave's daughter. When Mr. James' little girl was three years old, the master sold the child to a slave owner from a distant state.

For Staci, this information explained the hauntings at the

house, including the mystery painters and the two ghosts who hated each other, but it left one little mystery. . . *Why Ginger?*

Eventually, Staci guessed that the spirit of Mr. James was protecting the little girl from the evil ghost of Mr. Potter. Perhaps, Staci decided, the troubled kind slave found in Ginger a memory of his long-lost daughter, whom he never had a chance to enjoy.

—*Jaime Cherundolo*

About the writer

Jamie Cherundolo, of Newark, Delaware, is a junior English major at the University of Delaware. Like the main character in her story, Jamie spent much of her childhood shuttling back and forth between Newark, Maui and Hawaii. She describes herself as a lonely child who found refuge in reading, drawing and babysitting. At one time, she babysat two children named Tyler and Ginger, for whom the characters in this story are named. She said she enjoys writing and working with children.

"I'd like to dedicate this story to my 12th-grade English teacher and role-model Mary Ann Scarborough," Jamie said. "Thank you for always believing in me and making me feel like my efforts were worthwhile."

They Buried This Judge Twice in Dover

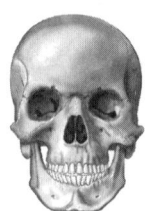

Dover, Delaware, is the First State's capital. It's also one of the most haunted sites on the Delmarva Peninsula, and stories of different spooky structures have been featured in other books in the Spirits Between the Bays series. Among Dover's list of recognized haunted houses are the Delaware Made General Store (written up in Vol. IX, *Phantom in the Bedchamber*), the Blue Coat Inn and John Dickinson Mansion (both in Vol. III, *Welcome Inn*) and Woodburn: The Governor's Mansion (featured in Vol. II, *Opening the Door*).

This well-known tale occurred in the open space area of the historic city known as The Green. It was here that a ghostly presence made a profound impact on the citizens and town during the middle of the 18th century.

Near midnight (it always seems to happen about that time) on a windy, stormy night, a citizen was crossing The Green, heading home to escape the troublesome weather.

With a start, the man stopped dead in his tracks, for he noticed a figure standing beneath a particular poplar tree. The startled man shielded his eyes from the wind, squinted and recognized the man under the tree. It was Chief Justice of Delaware Samuel Chew.

Unfortunately for the viewer, not the chief justice, it was well known that Samuel Chew had died many months before.

Turning quickly, the man who had sighted the departed justice took flight and, in the coming days, told his story to people throughout the city of Dover. Of course, the reactions ranged from polite nods and tolerance to downright ridicule and laughter.

The sighter was accused of being "in his cups" or having had too much of the "juice of the barley."

While the town was ignoring the stormy night sighting, another tale surfaced. This one from the mouth of a passing miller, who had not heard the first tale and who stated that he had seen Chief Justice Samuel Chew standing under the same poplar tree as the first witness.

This report was not as quickly dismissed. In fact, the result was a heightened sense of fear and concern. Stores began to close early, travelers stayed close to home and, horror of all horrors, the taverns in Dover were empty as the inside of a church on a Tuesday afternoon. Commerce was grinding to a halt, and the town officials decided something must be done.

As the plans to rid the town of the apparition were discussed, some mentioned that the reason for the ghost's presence may have to do with the treatment the chief justice had received from the populace.

During Judge Samuel Chew's court sessions, it was not uncommon to hear an unusually large amount of sneezing in his courtroom. "Ah-CHOO!" after "Ah-CHOO!" would be followed by smirks and smiles directed in the judge's direction. Others, who thought they were being clever, would demonstrate exaggerated chewing movements with their jaw and mouth as the judge looked out over the courtroom.

All this was a constant annoyance to the chief justice throughout his lifetime, but it was reported that during his funeral the level of sneezing and chewing intensified. Obviously, the ghost of Chief Justice Samuel Chew had seen the public mockery at his services, had disapproved of the treatment and had come back to punish the citizens of the town of Dover for their disrespect.

After some discussion, it was agreed that a new funeral service would be held, complete with mourners, and a procession to take place from the church to the base of the very same, old poplar tree where the miller and citizen had seen the white-wigged and black-robbed ghost of the town's dear departed chief justice.

Ghosts

As was prearranged, the mourners and procession arrived at the tree and surrounded the freshly dug grave. Then, under the watchful eye of minister, merchants and town officials, a more serious minded service was held to put to rest the ghost of the town's sorely missed and warmly loved Chief Justice Samuel Chew.

And from that day on, that particular ghost of the chief justice who died in 1743 has not appeared on The Dover Green or anywhere else—as far as we know.

Unending Drive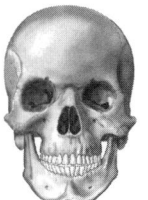

This strange story begins in the city limits of a mid-sized town in Georgia, late one Saturday night, actually quite early in the darkness of Sunday morning. That's when a majority of eerie and unexplained events usually occur.

Jane was driving home from a late night party. Having had one or two glasses of wine, she was being careful to avoid any contact with the law or other drivers, so she selected the back streets instead of the main roads through the sleepy town.

As Jane began to move forward after braking for a stop sign at a deserted intersection, she was surprised to see an odd looking official car pass slowly by on her left.

Jane recalled she was startled, particularly because she had been careful to watch out for other vehicles, especially marked police cars, because of her slightly buzzed state.

Nevertheless, there it was, a large green sedan, easing on by, silently, and moving past—almost noiselessly. It was both the silence of the car's passing and its dated style that initially caught Jane's attention.

"It was summer," she said. "Naturally, I had the windows down, my radio was off and I never heard the car approach. It just seemed to glide by next to me, without a sound. That was strange in itself, but then things got really scary."

Jane said her main objective was to get out of the area and avoid contact with authorities—and anyone else on the road at that hour. She just wanted to get home as quickly as possible.

"But I couldn't," she said, shaking her head. "After the car, which looked like an old military police car, went by, my car just seemed to move on its own. The steering wheel began to

Ghosts

turn and the gas pedal depressed and the brake wouldn't work. It was as if a magnet or some force was pulling my car along to keep up with the police car heading down the road in front of me. Thank God no one else was on the road, because I couldn't do a thing. I was along for the ride and my car just kept following the police car for about 15 minutes."

As the lead vehicle continued its roll through the streets, Jane sat holding onto her useless steering wheel and stared in horror at the moving police car. She recalled that after about three minutes she began to notice more details about the car she was following. It was so old, it was almost an antique.

"It looked like it was from an old movie, from the 1940s or '50s. The color was dark, but not black, more like an ugly green. And the shape of the car was rounded and fat, like a bubble. Not sharp and sleek like the cars from the '60s or '70s. I tried to focus on the license plate, but couldn't read it. Things looked fuzzy and foggy."

But she never got closer than about 100 feet. She recalled it was like she was being towed by a cable and she stayed the same distance away—for most of the time—until the end.

"We had gotten to the outskirts of town, and were going down a deserted back road. It was hardly more than a narrow lane wide," Jane said, "trees on all sides. I didn't know where I was heading and I was really starting to freak out. I began pounding on my horn. At least that worked. It let out a few loud blasts, three or four, and I noticed that the car in front seemed to respond. Its brake lights went on, very suddenly. But that's when everything happened all at once, and it was over in a flash, like a bolt of lightning or waking up from a bad dream."

Jane paused a minute or two to gather her thoughts.

"It was like you were on information overload," she said. Her eyes were closed for a second. She seemed to be trying to visualize the events that night so she could describe them again.

"I remember seeing everything at once, and, at the same time, I was trying to remember it all while I was also trying to figure out if everything was really happening to me at all. It's hard to explain. I mean, I was trying not to forget anything that was going on. But, at the same time, I was trying to keep from getting hurt or killed. I know it sounds crazy and confusing, but that's just the way it was."

Jane explained that after she began pounding on her horn, trying to get the police car's attention, the lead vehicle stopped suddenly and turned to the right—blocking the road in front of her. Her car, however, kept moving, heading straight for the car that was stopped sideways, blocking the narrow road.

She said she started screaming and shouting and putting her arms across her face, to shield herself from the injury and damage she was about to experience. But nothing horrible of a physical nature happened. She just glided through the other car like, she described, "just like a hot knife going through butter."

"When I threw my arms across my face," Jane said, "it was only seconds before my car was going to crash into the other one. Then, and I'll never know why, but for some reason, I lowered my arms so I could get a better look at what was going to happen. That sounds crazy, too, I know. But something told me I didn't have to worry, or maybe it was telling me that I should see what this was all about. I don't know which it was, but I do remember what I saw. I'll never forget it. Never."

Jane's car kept moving foward and the nose and hood pressed directly into the side of the olive drab police car. But there was no sound, no impact, no slowing of her speed. As her car passed through the interior and out the other side of the strange car she had been following, Jane saw the interior of the green car and the intense face of its driver.

She said the car had leather seats, an old-fashioned dashboard. Jane recalled the green and brown colors of the vehicle and, especially, the sad and mournful face of the driver, whose eyes stared straight into hers during the fraction of a second that they made contact.

"He was in uniform," Jane said. "It was a World War II style uniform, tan in color, and he had a white helmet. He was soldier, that's all I knew, but I had no idea why he was there or where he came from. But those eyes. It was like he was pleading for me to help him, like he was trapped. And I think I remember his lips being set in a sad shape. I don't know," Jane said, pausing, shaking her head. "Maybe I'm adding to the story as the years pass, thinking what I think may have happened really did. Like Al Gore does all the time, you know?" She laughed uneasily, obviously still bothered by that night years ago.

I started to ask a question, but she raised her hand and cut me off.

Ghosts

"Don't think," she said, forcefully, "that this didn't happen. I know it did. I wasn't drunk. I wasn't crazy. I might be confused as to whether that soldier smiled or not, but I know that somehow I was forced to follow that Army car. I can still see it spread across the road, and I saw the inside as I passed right through it. And I did, for damn sure, end up in a ditch on a back road in Georgia that summer night. There is no doubt about that, either."

When her car exited the phantom vehicle, she said she hit a hole and was afraid to get out. Her first instinct, after she realized she wasn't hurt, was to turn and hope the soldier was nearby and would come to her assistance.

But there was nothing there. No car. No one.

She was alone, at 2 o'clock in the morning, in a Georgia swamp.

She tried to move her car, but the wheels were stuck in the mud. After several tries, she made sure the doors were locked and the windows were cracked to let in air and she turned on the radio and waited for sunrise.

About 6:30 in the morning, she began walking up the road toward the highway.

"The hardest part," she said, "was passing the spot where I had last seen the Army car. I looked for tire marks going across the road, but all I found were mine. No trace of anything at all. When I passed that spot, I picked up the pace and never looked back until I got to the highway."

She hitched a ride into town, called a towing service and got her car back on Monday morning.

Jane never told anyone about her weekend from hell. She said she knew people would think she was drunk or crazy—probably both. But she had to find some reason, some explanation no matter how farfetched or bizarre, to help explain what she had experienced.

"I went to the library and asked the reference librarian for anything they had on local ghost stories," she said. "It was in August, and the lady at the desk asked, 'Isn't it a little early for Halloween, dear?' and she gave me a raised eyebrow look. But I didn't care. I was happy to have some place to get started."

She said there were a lot of the usual tales—stories on pirates and shipwrecks, of headless horsemen and ghosts from local lynchings. A bit frustrated, Jane said she was almost done with the file when she came across a small clipping. It was dated June 7, 1956, and only about three inches in size, but the words "ghostly army car" in the second paragraph caught her eye.

The headline and story read:

The ghost made me do it?

Norman Erlings was admitted to the Holy Name Hospital Sunday morning in a confused state following an automobile accident on Piney Swamp Road.

According to police reports, Mr. Erlings claimed that he was driven off the road by a "ghostly army car" that he and his pickup truck "passed right through" and then ended up in a gully.

Investigators on the scene reported no tracks, other than Mr. Erlings's truck tires markings, or any indication that another vehicle had been in the area.

Mr. Erlings was charged with reckless driving and fined $20. Investigators said they have given up the search for the phantom U.S. Army vehicle.

"I made a copy of the clipping and went to the phone book and called every Erlings listed," Jane said. "There were only three, and on the last call I was lucky to talk to Mr. Erlings's daughter, Sarah. She told me her father had died three years earlier, but that if I wanted to I could stop by for a visit."

Two days later, Jane spent nearly an hour with Sarah Erlings, in the old modest home where the woman had once lived with her parents. To her satisfaction, Jane said, Sarah did not seem surprised or bothered when asked about her departed father's experience with the "ghost car."

Jane tried to recall Sarah's coversation. She said the Erlings woman was adamant that her father had been telling the truth. "She told me that her 'Daddy swore to his dyin' day, he did, that he went through that there car like a train goin' downhill through a fog. Ain't nothin' stopped him, 'cept that ditch he ended up in—face down. Them po-leece, they all laughed when he done told them 'bout that ghost car. Said Daddy was liquored-up. But that weren't true. No way. 'Cause when he done tied one on, it lasted a whole full week, and when he come home that next mornin' he was sober as a damn judge on the bench. He hadn't had as much as a drop. An' his hands was just a shakin' like leaves in the wind when he told me and Mamma what he done saw.' "

Jane paused and smiled, obviously pleased that she was able to capture Sarah Erlings personality and dialog.

"Sarah was very kind with me, and she also said that I wasn't the only person who had stopped by to see her all these years."

Apparently, another woman that lived in the area had been the victim of a smiliar experience only two years before Jane's.

According to Jane, "Sarah told me she learned an interesting fact. It seems that the area where my car, and her father's truck and the other woman's car all had crashed—after driving through the ghost car, had been the back entrance to an abandoned military base that was used during World War II.

"The military police used to use that rear entrance late at night to take prisoners in and out of the compound. It's all gone now. Bulldozed down and overgrown with brush and vegetation. But," Jane said, pausing, "it's as good a reason as any, as far as I'm concerned."

Jane said the information on the old fort has helped her understand what probably occurred that summer night. But it hasn't stopped the nightmares, or the cold sweats, or eased her fear of driving alone after dark—especially on the side streets of that little Georgia town.

"When darkness starts to arrive," Jane said, "I head for home. I just don't go out alone, driving, anymore. I know it sounds crazy." She paused and forced a laugh. "And it probably seems nuts to a lot of people. But I don't care. All I want to do is make sure I don't see him or his car again. Don't get pulled along and swept away, like it happened that night.

"And the only way I can be sure is to stay home after dark—unless someone else is driving. Then, if it happened to them and I was there, in a way I'd be happy, or at least satisifed. Because then I would be sure I wasn't crazy, and that someone else I know saw it, too."

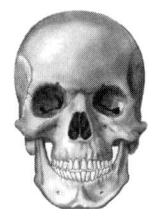

Slicer and Snooks

Each workday, which meant Monday through Saturday—with a day of rest on the Lord's Day, provided no emergency occurred that needed attention—Art Slicer worked his family's 200-acre farm, located in the southeast corner of Queen Anne's County on Maryland's Eastern Shore.

Even though his name was Art, nobody called him that. He just went by the name Slicer, had been that way for almost forever. It started up when he was in first grade and now, 68 years later, that was the only name to which he responded.

About two years ago, Slicer had what they call a life-changing event, and immediately afterwards, he hadn't been himself. Thing was, the old farmer just couldn't get over the accidental death of his faithful huntin' dog Snooks. Up until that misfortune, Snooks and Slicer had been inseparable. Wherever the farmer went, Snooks was close at hand.

Working, fishing or just sitting on the back porch—whatever Slicer did, there was Snooks, walking nearby or resting at his master's feet. It was as if the dog had the ability to get into Slicer's mind and know in advance what the farmer needed or what the old man was going to do.

Only one time did Snooks make the wrong decision, and that error proved fatal. But who would have known that an accident was going to occur?

"That's why they call it an accident," Slicer said, sitting on his back porch, sipping a warm can of Bud. "We had gone out huntin' quail," Slicer began to explain, shaking his head as he recalled the event. "Snooks was out in the field, flushing out the game, and me, I was waitin' in the high grass, ready to shoot down the game when they took flight. The worstest part of the damn tragedy, I tell ya, was there was no way it should of happened—not to somebody like me, an ol' hunter an' a ol' reliable hound".

Slicer had nailed a plump quail with one shot, and Snooks was heading back with the feathered prize in its mouth. Suddenly, Slicer stepped in a hole. Unable to hold his balance, the farmer began to fall and his reflexes squeezed the trigger of his old two-barrel shotgun—the weapon without a safety.

The explosion of shot went off just before the farmer's shoulder hit the ground, with the blast hitting Snooks' face and chest, less than five feet away.

"By the time I was able to toss aside the gun an' crawl over to Snooks," Slicer said, "he jest gave outta whimper. An' I caught a glimpse of Snook's lids closing over them large, sad, black eyes."

Slicer paused and shook his head, then he added, "I swear to ya, that the first time in nearly 10 years that I let outta a tear. Hadn't felt that much pain since Martha was lowered in the family plot behind the farmhouse."

But, surprisingly, Slicer's mood changed and he seemed to recover quite quickly, regaining his composure.

"That's cause Snooks ain't gone," he said. "Damn dog's still here. Right on the porch, now, sure as we are speakin'."

My look of confusion betrayed the unasked questions in my brain, and Slicer, catching my quandary, began to explain.

"I got me a genuine ghost dog, here," he said proudly. Then added that Snooks had arrived at Slicer's doorstep soon after his wife, Martha's, funeral. A neighbor had hoped that the dog would help get Slicer through the difficult lonely days immediately following Martha's death. The animal had done the trick. But when it was gone as suddenly and surprisingly as it had arrived, and it being Slicer's fault, he began carrying the guilt of Snooks' death around his neck like a 50-pound bag of blame that he would never be able to shed.

"The offers came fast and furious as soon as word got out that Snooks was gone," Slicer said. "But, at 75, I was too damned old to be bogged down with tranin' another young pup. I told 'em to jest leave me be!"

Of course, Slicer being a master of direct, face-to-face communication, folks did as they were told. No new four-legged friend was delivered to Slicer's door. Plus, after several attempts at neighborly, hot casserole deliveries were rejected, rarely did the two-legged variety of caller stop by to offer a hand.

Folks knew a stubborn old cuss when they saw one, and that's what Slicer had become. He would probably die out there on his farm alone one night, but that's just the way it would have to be. Neighbors with good intentions could only be run off so many times before they headed for the high road and never came back.

"I got used to bein' out here alone," he said. "Jest me an' my mem'ries. No bother. No fuss. No one to please or tend to. But I sure did miss that dog. Still feel bad about that shootin'. But I guess Snooks got over it, quick enough, though."

Snooks had come back, Slicer said, and saved the farmer's life not once, but twice.

"I know you're thinkin', 'This old coot's been out in the field too long without a cap,' but I tell ya, it's the God's honest truth. Sometimes, the damn dog licks my hand with his tongue and when I lift it up, the back of my hand is wet all over. Swear to the Lord!"

It was six months after Snooks had been shot and Slicer was steering his tractor back toward the barn to get in out of an approaching storm.

"Wind was blowin' like it was the Wizard of Oz tornado a comin' on right fast," he said. "Branches flyin', crops pullin' up by the roots right outta the soil. Was a mean one."

He was about a half-mile from home when the speed of the wind got so bad Slicer could hardly see.

"That's when I hit the grove, right down there," he said, pointing toward a creek bed and thick stand of trees behind the farmhouse. "I was holdin' on for dear life. White knucklin' that tractor wheel as I hit the treeline. I knew it was dangerous goin' in there with the storm, big branch mighta gone an' fallen on me. Woulda knocked me flat out—or even worse. But," he asked, pausing, "what the hell was my choice? If I got off it an' left the tractor out there it coulda been blowed to the next town

Ghosts

an' back. I hadta get it inta the barn. So I gunned that sucker, tryin' to blaze on through the grove an' make it up the hill to the barn. That's when she got me."

"The storm?" I asked.

"No," he said. "Snooks. My ghost dog."

Slicer said that when he was about half way through the grove, the branches started falling all around him—to the rear, front and sides. Several hit the fenders and rear of the machine. He looked ahead to get a bearing on the roadway and closed his eyes to keep out the dust.

"There was no way I could see where I was goin'," he said. "Woulda needed a pair o' them swimmin' glasses to see in front of ya. So I tried to keep movin'. Then I heard a crack, right up above. Sounded like a lightnin' bolt or a shot from a deer rifle jest over my head."

Pausing, Slicer shook his head, then continued. "I knew I was gone, then. Realized in a flash that somethin' had hit a big oak and that it was gonna fall right on top a me. I couldn't move. Froze. Let up on the gas pedal and braced my body for the hit I was sure was gonna come. Then, like outta nowhere, I get knocked outta my seat from the side.

"I was expectin' to get crushed from the top, an' instead I get slammed in my left shoulder. It was like a football player, or some hockey guy, took his whole damn body and layed into me. In a flash I was on the ground, layin' beside the front wheel of the tractor. And, at that moment, when I was tryin' to get myself upright, two things happened. A massive tree limb, musta been 18 inches thick, hits the seat o' my tractor—right were I was sittin' only a second ago. Plus, some force is holdin' down my chest so I can't get back up. An' believe me, I was tryin' hard to stand myself up on my feet an' move off from the ground."

I waited for Slicer to continue. At this point there was nothing to ask. Silence was golden, letting him gather his thoughts.

"It was Snooks for certain," he said, casually. "Was there to save my behind. I's sure of that as I am that this is Tuesday night an' I's sittin' on my porch with a cold one. No doubt at all in my mind. That damn dog came back, saved my life that day. Lord God be my judge."

The second incident occurred when Slicer traveled to

Salisbury to get some engine parts and made a wrong turn or two, ending up in a bad section of town.

After driving his Chevy pickup into a dead end street, he tried to back up the vehicle and turn around. As he turned his head to the left, to look into his rear view mirror, a teenager was at his side with a pistol only five inches from Slicer's forehead.

"I been in the Army, worked in the fields and had accidents and been scared before," Slicer said, "but never like this. I knew for damn sure that I was gonna be payin' St. Peter a house call. No doubt. My days was over. I froze up. Wasn't no use fightin' this one. That little bastard had the drop on me and nothin' I was gonna do or say was gonna make him go away or change his damn mind.

"I'll never forget his eyes. They was big and black. His skin was black, his eyes was black and that gun was silver, with a black handle grip. But that boy's eyes was cold as January ice in the bay. No fear in them, like he was gonna shoot me whether I gave him what he wanted or not. I was a dead man for sure."

Obviously, Slicer didn't die. In fact, he never even found out what the boy wanted—even thought it probably was the truck or money.

Snooks struck again.

"As that boy is about to blow me away, I close my eyes. Gave up. Then, I hear this screamin' an' the damn bastard is rollin' around on the ground like he's havin' a fit. St. Vitus' Dance or whatever, I don't know what the hell's goin' on. I think he's havin' some kinda seizure. Then, I realize he's yellin' at me to get 'em off. 'Get 'em off! Call off your dog!' he's shoutin' as he's bein' pulled an' dragged an' bitten all over.

"That's when I realize it's Snooks again. He's back to watch over me like before, in the tornado. 'cept this time, the dog come along for the ride to the big city. So I yell, 'SNOOKS!' An' the tusslin' stops, an' that little bastard was gonna rob me stops movin'. But he's there, real still, holdin' his arm an' chest, like he's scared to death. Hell, I guess he was, since my ghost dog's been biting 'em an' he can't even see what it was attackin' the hell outta him an' all."

Slicer said he lowered the tailgate, called out for Snooks to get back into the truck and drove off, leaving the boy huddled up in a moaning ball on the ground.

Ghosts

"But I took his gun," Slicer said, opening a drawer from the cabinet at his side. Tossing it onto the table between us, he said, "I know to you it ain't proof. You're thinkin' that maybe I keep it to fool people about my tall tales. But I don't have no time for games. Don't care if folks believe me or don't. I's alive. I got the gun, an' most of all, I still got Snooks. So, that's my story."

Slicer paused and leaned back in his chair for a moment. I waited him out, figured he had more to say.

"I guess ol' Snooks might be good for one more life-savin' event. Then, it'll be my time," Slicer said, smiling. "But I tell ya, it's strange and comfortin', havin' that ol' dog around. Sometimes, I swear I can jest smell it when he's nearby. An' if I hold my hand real still, danglin' down toward the floor, like now," he said, looking at his old wrist, waving gently, "I jest might feel him nuzzle on by, rest with me a short bit. Then, sometimes, like I told ya, he'll give a good ol' lick and leave his mark. Ain't nothin' better than that. Nothin' at all in life."

I thanked Slicer for the story, and the refreshment, then headed across the lane to my car. As I closed the driver's door, I looked up at the old farmer on the porch and waved. He raised his can of Bud and signaled a friendly reply, then rested his body against the rear of the porch chair.

After starting my engine, I thought I heard a bark. But that was probably just wishful thinking, hoping for some evidence that Snooks might be in the area and give me a tangible sliver of his mystical existence. No such luck.

But a final glance toward Slicer indicated that he looked happy, content, at peace with himself. And that really was all that mattered. But I swear he was leaning down, looking toward the porch floor and waving something away with his free hand. Maybe a fly or bee that was buzzing nearby. Or perhaps Slicer was rubbing the soft coat on the back of his faithful, invisible friend, who had let the guilty farmer know that it realized its death had been an accident.

Who knows?
Who can be sure?
But I like to think so.

Preserving the Past

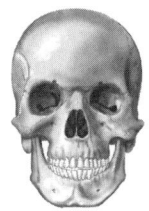

If the expression, "They've been together forever," applied to any married couple, it was Custis and his devoted wife, Rebecca. Even though they had spent what seemed like a lifetime together, and usually agreed on nearly everything, at this particular moment they both were in a sour mood.

The cause of their aggravation was external activity beyond their control that was occurring not far from the mansion of their centuries-old family plantation. For weeks, throughout the day and even sometimes in early evening, the sounds of heavy machinery at work could be heard in the distance. Powerful, orange, oversized earthmovers rammed their wide-tooth shovels into the Delmarva soil, gobbling up acre upon acre of scenic farmland. The metal monsters' mission was to clear a very straight and narrow path to accommodate yet another high-speed roadway (not very far from a similar one that had been built only years earlier).

"Where are all these people coming from and where are they all rushing to and from?" Rebecca snapped, knowing that her husband would give her the same answer he always did.

"From another time and place, and they all intend to pass through our area as speedily as possible. But, they all will . . . "

"Spare me, for I know the rest, Custis! '...arrive at the same place, and simply have to wait for attention, for they are far too many,' " Rebecca said, finishing her husband's explanation.

"Then if you know the answer," her husband challenged, "why do you continue to ask? No matter how often you inquire of me, the facts of this matter, I say again, will not change."

Ghosts

Silence dominated the next 15 seconds, and then Rebecca spoke in a soft but worried voice. "They are getting closer, Custis, much closer each day. You are certainly well aware that they will be upon us within a short span of time—with no regard for our home, heritage or our respected position in the community."

Custis did not respond. Indeed, he was aware that the approaching portion of the Rapid Beach Route, which would connect Wilmington, Delaware, to the state's southern beaches, was heading straight for Chatfield Manor, their historic homestead. He also knew there was absolutely nothing he or anyone in the family could do to stop, or even slow, the inevitable advance of progress. Therefore, Custis and Rebecca and their entire family were scheduled to be relocated.

"The Chatfields have been here since two years after the original settlement at Lewestown," Rebecca said, stating the obvious. "This is our ancestral home! By God, I do not intend to be forced out without resistance!"

"We have no choice," Custis replied. His voice was weary, for the same conversation had been repeated almost verbatim for the last six months. "They ignore our situation and treat us as if we don't even exist. You have to accept reality, my dear, the plans have been approved, the turnpike is moving forward."

"They can alter the route if they desire," Rebecca snapped. "Directing the new roadway only one-fourth of a mile to the west will allow us to continue unmolested. Then, we would be safe, undisturbed—except for the passing vehicle noise. But, we've learned to cope with that for all of these years. We shall adjust our habits accordingly again."

"Stop it! Please!" Custis shouted, voicing his frustration with his wife's incessant complaints. "It serves no serious purpose to restate your objections to what certainly will occur. Even our preservationist friends have tried in vain to alter the route. They, too, have been defeated, and soundly so, in both the courtroom and in the latest newspaper polls. You must acknowledge reality. People do not care. They want convenience. Therefore, Chatfield Manor is doomed, and so are we."

But Rebecca still had some fighting spirit left. Slowly, she began to unfold her plan, realizing that if she announced her objective too quickly her husband would ignore her logic and refuse to participate. However, since her youth she was considered to be among the most manipulative and strong-willed of the Chatfield clan. Knowing her talent at manipulation, she spoke with a combination of confidence and cunning.

"Since before the Revolution," Rebecca said, "the rattle of gold coins in a cloth pouch would determine who would dance and who would sit and enjoy the performance. In this instance," she said, confidently, "I do not intend to perform."

"There are no other options," Custis said, now openly annoyed with the length of a discourse that was headed nowhere.

"Wrong," she said, smoothly, "you, my darling, must pay an evening visit to Terrance."

"NO!" Custis snapped, without hesitation. His reply was automatic and firm. "That is impossible!"

"Nothing is impossible if there remains a chance that we could save Chatfield."

"NO! This discussion is over. I command you to stop, now!"

"You can command your servants and your children," Rebecca snarled, "but you, and no other form of man, will ever dare command what I think or say." After a brief pause, she added, "Especially one like you, devoted Custis, who had the rare fortune to marry into the Chatfields and have blatantly sucked from its bounty for so many years."

Custis remained still.

"And now," Rebecca stressed, "as I said, I have decided that you must pay Terrence a call."

"I do not approve of the way he operates," Custis said, "and, more importantly, he is beneath our class."

Seething, Rebecca snapped back, "He has power! All the power we need to change the course of the approaching storm. And, as for his station," she said, pausing, "I would rather stand beside a man with authority and lack of pedigree than one who claims a multitude of useless titles but who lacks basic courage."

Ignoring the insults, Custis replied, "He will want something substantive in return. He always does. And the thought of kneeling before his throne, supplicating myself for . . . "

"For the sake of preserving our heritage," Rebecca hissed. "If I were able, I would approach him myself and promise to do whatever he asked to save Chatfield."

Ghosts

"Then you go!" Custis shouted. "Do as you will!"

"You know he will not see me. In dealings of business, that pompous potentate speaks only with men. It is his way. It always has been."

"His prideful, toplofty, ostentatious way!" Custis spat the words out of his mouth as if they were hot coals.

"But the alternative, my dear Custis," Rebecca cooed, "will hang on your misguided pride. When you and I and our children and family are scattered to the winds, separated forever, let the burden rest on your damned soul when our mansion is razed and the new road cleaves us apart, limb from limb."

As Custis mulled his wife's last threatening remark, Rebecca added, "There is nothing I would not do, no humiliation I would not endure, to keep us as we are—safe, close and together. Now, go to Terrence."

"He'll want something, that is quite certain."

"Pay him homage," she replied. "Offer him thanks, acknowledge his power. Is that so difficult for you?"

"Yes, it is. For I will be forced to give my word that I will respond when he calls. Whenever and for whatever purpose, with no questions or hesitancy."

"Nothing is without cost," Rebecca said. "My ancestors arrived in this land before this young country was a nation. They placed their lives, their spirits, their sweat, hearts and bodies into Chatfield soil. My bloodline formed this nation, and their descendants fought to preserve it. I refuse to allow your masculine pride to stand in our way. Go, and promise him whatever you must to secure our security."

Only after layers of darkness and patches of rolling fog swallowed the surface of the Appoquinimink River, did Custis begin his difficult and painful journey. Silently, he moved among the shadows. To avoid being seen, he traveled below and along the woodline of the main roads, across marshland and moors, through narrow paths and over gravel lanes, until he reached the secluded manse of Terrence.

Two black cloaked guards escorted the weak and exhausted visitor into the dark paneled study that overlooked the inky waters of the swiftly flowing Delaware. A sliver of moonlight was all that illuminated the unlit room. Standing off to the side of a half-shuttered window, Terrence stared at the visitor.

"Your mistress sent you." His voice was calm yet firm, the sound of one who knew he had the upper hand.

"How did you know?" Custis asked, somewhat nervous.

"I know all," the host said, smiling. "Word travels rapidly among the breathless clans. I command the services of unseen eyes and unnoticed ears. My sources exist in the highest treetops and extend into the bowels of Mother Earth. Of course, every source has its price. And, as you are aware, I pay handsomely but rightly demand much."

Custis waited. Terrence took several steps forward and extended a thin, bony hand.

The visitor, who would soon make a request in the name of the entire Chatfield clan, knelt, bowed his head and kissed the powerful one's black onyx ring.

"I will need much compensation to deliver what you have come to request," Terrence said.

Surprised, Custis began to speak, "How do you . . . ."

Waving off the kneeling figure's comment in mid-sentence, Terrence continued. "What work did you perform in years past? Of what venture or skill were you acquainted?"

"I toiled as a blacksmith by trade. After marrying into the Chatfields, I moved into farming, tobacco farming."

"I have no need for the evil weed, but at some point I may be in search of special implements. You will, of course, be at my disposal from this day hence and fashion them to my exact specifications, without question. When I request, it is not so, but in truth a command. All of your other personal and family affairs will cease immediately. For you will serve me, unconditionally, and do my bidding from this day hence. When I issue my call, you ask no questions, only comply. I gather you find these terms acceptable?"

Nodding, Custis agreed, thinking Terrence's payment was much less than he and Rebecca has expected. He began to feel proud that he had gotten what his wife needed for such a small promise.

After a few awkward moments of silence, Terrence spoke again. "One more small demand," he said, smiling as he continued. "Your bride, Lady Rebecca, shall visit me, twice monthly, and remain several days to serve as my hostess, to do my bidding as I see fit." Then a broad smile consumed the phantom's face. "Agreed?"

Although shocked, Custis responded quickly, nodded in agreement. He did not want Terrence to change his mind nor realize that Custis' essence was becoming consumed with fear. His wife would not be happy. But, Custis thought somewhat happily, his overbearing spouse had sent him to enact the bargain and resolve it he had—at her expense. If she moaned, let the anguish be on her haughty, domineering soul.

"So be it!" Terrence announced, slapping his hands together. Then, he pulled Custis closer and embraced the hapless visitor who had just sold what shreds remained of his ragged soul, and that of his spouse, to the appalling tall beast in the black wardrobe. As they hugged, the master bit his fangs into the ear of his new associate, ripping off Custis' left lobe.

The shocked victim tried to pull away, but was held fast by Terrence's strength. While in the clutching embrace, Terrence whispered into Custis' ripped and ragged ear, "It is done. Tell your mistress that she and her lineage will rest safe and well for many generations to come. The roadway will be moved, Chatfield will not be disturbed, but never forget that you and she—along with all your heirs and ancestors—are at my disposal for all time."

Custis did not know how to respond.

"Say the words 'So be it, Master,' " Terrence commanded, his voice a whispering hiss.

"So be it, Master," Custis whispered.

"It is done," Terrence said. "Now," he added, pushing away from his newly acquired serf, "from what sources did you secure the energy to materialize and make this journey. I know you did not possess enough stamina from you and your mistress alone?"

"We drained the essence of two generations beyond ourselves, Master. They will be indisposed for a period of a fortnight, but it was their duty. With luck, there should be enough strength for my return journey, but only if I am able to leave before the sunrise and keep to the shadows. Otherwise . . . "

"Otherwise," Terrence continued, smiling, "you will perish with the light. If that occurs, although a tragedy for you, it would not be beneficial regarding our bargain. But then, whether the roadway passes over, under, around and through Chatfield would no longer be of your concern. Correct?"

Custis nodded slowly, then whispered, "I would hope for my mistress' sake, that you would honor our agreement."

Laughing, Terrence clapped his claws and summoned his guards. "Place our new recruit, Master Custis, here, into my best vehicle, the one with the tinted glass, and deposit his sorry soul at Chatfield with all haste. I want him well cared for and rested when I call upon his services."

Bowing, Custis took his leave.

Nodding, Terrence smiled and said, "You will be at your homestead well before the rays of light break above the river's horizon. There, I need you to rest and wait. Until we meet again!" Terrence turned and walked into the darkest corner of the room and disappeared.

Two nights later, a rotund, white-haired visitor arrived to speak with Terrence in the same dark chamber where the phantom conducted his arrangements with Custis—and thousands of others who had sought his assistance over the centuries.

For more than 70 years, Peter Lynch had served in nearly every elected and appointed office in the county—as chief commissioner, chief executive, register of deeds, recorder of wills, sheriff, coroner, building inspector and tax collector. More importantly, he had been chairman for both major parties—working the wards, fixing elections and making sure the dead got several extra chances to vote.

Most of his friends and associates were taking a dirt nap. Only a handful of those who had been around when Peter Lynch arrived on the political scene were still breathing, and they were doing so with the help of oxygen tanks or ventilators. Since he had been out of the public eye for more than 15 years, average citizens thought the old time ward boss was dead. But Peter the Great was very much alive and well, looking incredibly fit for a man who had to be in his late 90s. Somewhere he must have found the Fountain of Youth, or made a deal with the devil.

It was not an exaggeration to state that he was the most feared public servant, the one who knew where all the skeletons

Ghosts

were buried. And Peter the Great could keep them hidden or unearth them as needed to get what he wanted accomplished. Every politician in the state—from every party—had to pay monetary homage to Peter the Great before achieving elected or appointed office.

The old timer still wielded significant power, but he conducted his transactions in the shadows.

Tonight he was on familiar turf, in Terrence's office, for the phantom figure has been one of Peter's business colleagues for many years—decades, in fact. The political dealmaker was in high spirits, for he knew that he would never leave Terrence's abode empty handed. An arrangement was in the making and considerable funds would change hands, with a substantial amount landing in Peter's bulging coffers.

Clasping cold, shriveled hands, the associates nodded, smiled and got down to business.

"I need a serious accommodation, Peter," Terrence announced.

"It will cost you, of course," Peter said, smiling. His old teeth were yellow, even in the darkness of the room they looked odd, inhuman, stained and rotted. A short breath of stench escaped his puffy lips.

"Of course," Terrence said, waving his long, thin fingers as if he were pushing aside the air. "What is money, but to use, abuse, distribute and reclaim."

"That is the attitude of one with significant amounts of money," Peter stated. "Those with limited capital are not as cavalier."

Terrence smiled, then continued, explaining that the roadway now under construction must be redirected to preserve the historic structures on Chatfield Manor.

"That decrepit hovel is about to fall over," Peter said. "The owners did not even take the time to argue against the route at the public meeting. Now, after construction is under way, these fools want to have us make modifications. That will be direly difficult."

Peter let the last statement hang in the air to allow its message to alert Terrence that the price of request would be high. After a few silent moments, he continued. "But, it can be done, of course, if I pay off the county commissioners, state inspectors, construction crew bosses, owners, suppliers, transportation crew engineers, sewer and water . . . ."

"ENOUGH!" Terrence snapped. "You've made your point, old friend. But, as you said, it can be done. Now, it is late. Let us cut to the chase. How much coinage will have to change hands?"

Peter the Great loved this moment in the negotiation. It was at the age-old crossroad of need and supply, demand and price, give and take, which he excelled. He was shrewd, knowing he must be careful not to ask too little—for fear of not reaching what his adversary had already prepared to give. But, neither could he demand too much, for then he would be forced to retreat to a smaller number and, for a being with his years of experience and knowledge, to do so would be a personal humiliation and defeat.

Closing his eyes, the old politician imagined a figure. Stared at it in his mind, visualized the large dollar sign and the healthy six digits that followed. Then, silently, without moving his chapped, ruby-red, oversized, pouty lips, he shouted the amount inside his head, screamed it to himself to summon confidence. In secret, to himself, he repeated his wish number twice, three times, before he shared it with his rival.

Finally, Peter opened his eyes, stared at Terrence, and announced through his hoarse, low voice, "It can be done, but I will need $250,000. If I walk out with that amount in cash tonight, construction will cease tomorrow, by noon."

"Done!" Terrence said, without hesitation, tossing a leather pouch filled with gold coins across the table.

Opening the soft red case, Peter the Great shook the 12 oversized golden discs onto the wooden surface and, lifting it by its edge held up one of the valuable discs. Amazed at its sterling condition, the fine detailed etchings, he knew the treasures would be prized additions to his collection.

"Each one is worth at least $25,000. If you are able to gain more and arrive at an excess payment, place it on my account," Terrence said, "for I am sure we will meet soon to execute another transaction."

"Of course," Peter said, rising from his stool and heading toward the door. Then, turning suddenly, he asked, "Who are these fools that want to preserve what's left of that old manor house and grounds?"

Ghosts

Terrence waited a moment, the said, "Distant relatives who have a sentimental attachment to the old homestead. Fools, I agree. But, if not for them, you would not be walking off with the fool's gold."

Laughing, Peter nodded and then said, "I'm sure you are making a jest, about this being 'fool's gold,' fake gold, my friend."

"By all means, my long trusted colleague," Terrence said, smiling. "I beg your pardon. What a poor attempt at humor, for it is my error, indeed. Rest well knowing your payment is in fine legal tender."

After Peter drove off in his 1970s-vintage white Cadillac Eldorado. Terrence instructed his driver to prepare his black limousine. Within 20 minutes, he was standing in a weed-infested driveway. He looked up at the sagging portico and then stared at the worn slats of the broken steps leading to the massive entry doors of Chatfield Manor.

Graffiti, along with trash and garbage were cluttered about, marring the front of the manse.

Pointing to the side of the derelict mansion, he instructed his assistant to light the broken and overgrown path toward the rear of the building. About 100 feet behind the back kitchen door, at the crest of a knoll overlooking Appoquinimink Creek, rested the family graveyard.

The servant in the black hooded cloak shoved open the rusted iron gate that led into the Chatfield plot, marked off by ornate iron fencing. Several of the stones had been overturned, pushed aside and destroyed by vandals who had left evidence of their evening visits in the form of crushed beer cans and empty wine bottles.

Terrence's thick-soled boots stepped over broken shards of glass, the crushing sound disappearing quickly in the damp night air.

"The fog is approaching from the creek," Terrence said. "Here, bring the light so I may see the names on the old stones."

Leaning forward, the Master and his aide moved the glowing lantern from one grave marker to the next, reading the old inscriptions quickly. Most of the scalloped granite markers were well worn, making it hard to distinguish the letters and dates. Finally, the shorter man grunted, pointing toward two markers resting side by side.

The taller one, the man's, was tilted forward at an odd angle. No doubt its bent over position allowed the stone's carved inscription to be preserved longer than many of the other tombstones nearby.

Terrence placed the palm of his hand against the ground in front of the headstone. It was warm to the touch, indicating that the longtime resident had recently entered the soil and returned to his plot.

The woman's marker stood erect, straight and proud, perhaps informing visitors that the grave's occupant had appeared in that manner in life—direct, straightforward and serious, all well-known Chatfield family traits.

As the yellow glow made contact with the weathered gray stone, Terrence read the words aloud:

> *Custis Wellford, husband of Rebecca Chatfield,*
> *proud father and fair merchant.*
> *Born in Blackbird Crossing,*
> *May 14th, 1703*
> *Died at Chatfield Manor,*
> *Oct. 30th, 1746*
>
> *Waiting in a holy stillness, wrapt in sleep.*

Moving to the adjacent marker, Terrence resumed reading:

> *Rebecca Chatfield Wellford, loving wife and*
> *proud mistress of the Manor.*
> *Born at Chatfield Manor,*
> *June 2nd, 1715*
> *Died at Chatfield Manor,*
> *September 24, 1762*
>
> *Remember me, as you pass by.*
> *As you are now, so once was I.*
> *As I am now, so you must be.*
> *Prepare for death and follow me.*

Ghosts

Terrence knelt at the foot of Rebecca's gravesite, lowered his body and pressed his ear to the grassy surface. After a few moments, he smiled, enjoying the snippet of conversation that he was able to hear between the domineering mistress and the maltreated husband she had sent to do her bidding.

Obviously, he thought to himself, the state of affairs within the Chatfield plot is no longer peaceful and serene. But, he mused as he rose and walked toward his vehicle, nothing comes without some form of payment. And even those who think death is the end of all of life's irritations may be in for a delightfully monstrous surprise.

Not Your Average Old Haunted House

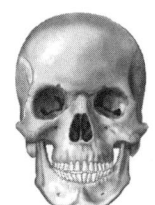

Years ago, there was an especially active "haunted house" within the town boundaries of Delaware City. From the large Victorian's top floor, the original residents could see the waters of the swiftly flowing Delaware, the scenic riverway that has played a vital role in the military, transportation and economic history of the country.

During the last 400 years, the Delaware River has hosted pirates and patriots, noblemen and thieves, 20th century tourists and 19th century Confederate prisoners. On its waves, British gunships have sailed and underneath its surface, German U-boats have sought their prey. And along its banks, villages, towns and cities have grown and written interesting histories of their own.

Many believe spirits remain near historic sites because old and restored buildings, antiques, narrow streets and preserved landmarks offer a receptive and familiar setting for these lingering phantoms. Certainly, they find these sites much more welcome and comfortable than sterile accommodations in modern cities with structures made of aluminum, plastic and composite metals.

Ghosts

That's why you find many more ghost stories at places like Fort Delaware, New Castle, Gettysburg, Woodburn: Delaware's Governor's Mansion, in old cemeteries and on wooden sailing ships.

Really now, how many ghost stories have you heard taking place at Taco Bell or McDonald's?

Therefore, what better town than historic, hospitable Delaware City for our spirit guests to linger. A major portion of the downtown area was named an historic district and listed on the National Register of Historic Places in December 1983. The architecture ranges from the early 1800s to the early 1900s. Structures that housed old inns, hotels and taverns remain from their glory days when the city was a major stop for travelers along the C & D Canal.

Since there are so many ghost stories in this small river city, those familiar with the area will wonder if this particular ghost house is one of the stately residences on Washington Street, or might it be one of the smaller-sized, but equally attractive, homes on nearby Adams Street.

Could the location of much unexplained activity be one of the many well-kept residences with manicured yards along wide and well-traveled Clinton Street, the main thoroughfare leading directly to the town park and dock?

While I cannot provide the specific address, nor any clue to which house is the keeper of these tales, I suggest the reader rule out the following better known town ghost havens.

- Our haunted home is not the old sea captain's residence that's said to have a cellar tunnel leading to the river. Through this passageway, it's believed, a crafty old sailor carted his contraband and stolen goods.

- It's also not the apartment where the ghost cat teases startled dogs. This activity still occurs, causing frustrated canines to charge after the phantom cat and crash their excited snouts against the wall as the feline spirit races through the solid plaster partition.

- Likewise, forget about any of the homes on Henry Street. In this area reports surface about the sound of footsteps belonging to the phantom marching regiment—which used to carry supplies from the old railroad station on Jefferson Street back to Fort DuPont.

- Nor are we discussing the mansion where Confederate phantoms appear beside a well-tended family boneyard. Rebel bodies were buried "under" legitimate family graves after sick prisoners in hiding had expired in the cellar of the hosts, secret Southern sympathizers.
- It's not even one of the houses where residents still hear the sound of Irish laborers, singing Old Country tunes in the night mist as they repeat their digging along the original route of the Chesapeake and Delaware Canal.

Old-timers and students of history know there are countless other specters roaming the town—including the spirit of the man who drowned in the old canal lock, the ghost of the child who died while ice skating on the frozen river, apparitions who peer out second-floor windows of shops along Clinton Street and the restless fireman who died from injuries while fighting the blaze that nearly destroyed the watertown in the late 1800s.

But the ghosts in this particular haunted home in DC (that's what some of the locals call Delaware City) are a bit more contemporary than those historic specters already mentioned. And, some think, a bit more frightening. Read on, and then you can decide for yourself.

Even after the large single home had been turned into several apartments, in the 1940s, it remained attractive. "Architecturally pleasing" is how people described it. The interior modifications had carved up the larger rooms, but to passers-by along the street, the house still looked like a large, one-family residence.

It also appeared comfortable, inviting and homey on the inside—at first—but after a short time, some new tenants began to observe things that they realized shouldn't occur.

Items became lost then reappeared, causing the owners to question their powers of observation. Doors opened and closed, apparently under their own power. Footsteps originated in seemingly vacant apartments. And apparitions appeared often, especially in two apartments in the front portion of the building.
It was a home of strange events, housing strange entities. And, as in any small town, word got out and interesting stories started to make the rounds. Naturally, the ghost tales grew, and those incidents that were stranger than life became even larger when

connected to the afterlife. Who knows where the truth ends and the embellishment begins—but one thing was certain, everyone knew the house was haunted.

"We didn't go into that old house," Gus said, shaking his lowered head back and forth. "It used to look pretty good years ago. Then, it just went an' gone straight on downhill. What a shame. But you won't even get me to go onto that old lot where it used to be, neither, not even today. Still a haunted place as far as I believe. I wouldn't even go through that house to pick it clean when its time came, when it was gone for good. No way then an' no way even now."

The old waterman had spent his entire life in DC and was more than willing to spend an afternoon on the banks of the old canal, spinning tales and sharing ghost stories. Like most old-timers, it wasn't hard to get him to recall—and tell an interested visitor—strange events that had happened some while back. "These days," Gus said, "ya don't find too many folks who wanna know about this stuff. They got themselves fixated on *history*," he paused after stressing the last work, "but, they seem to leave out the *story* part, an' to me, that's the best part, stories. They think that everything has to be written down an' come from the papers or books or the like. Hell! I got everything I need to know right up here," he said, pointing toward the top of his head. "An' if I forget it, then it ain't worth rememberin'. An', even at my old age, I can always make it up an' get pretty damn close to what happened."

So, I asked Gus, what he remembered about the big old haunted house.

"Lotsa tales, tall, long an' short," he replied without hesitation. "Some ya'll believe right off, others ya won't be sure of. But, I don't care if ya believe me or not. Don't make no difference, 'cause I know it's true. That's all that counts."

As I continued to press Gus for details, a friend of his came by and my source got up and moved off to a nearby alley, out of earshot, to talk some "crit'cal personal business." After 10 minutes he returned and showed me a few tickets that he had just bought for the annual Watermen's Lodge Wild Game Dinner.

"Wanna go?" Gus asked, shoving two tickets in my direction. "Ya gotta get tickets early. Can't wait, ya know. Real popular shindig. They go faster than an' eel in a oilslick."

"What do they have to eat?" I asked.

"Delaware City surf an' turf," Gus said, a wide grin spreading across his gaunt, stubble-cheeked face.

"Really?"

"Yep. Real good eatin'. City surf an' turf. That's catfish and muskrat. Home cooked and drippin' with lotsa gravy. Damn good eatin'. I only got 12 tix to sell. Fundraiser, ya know. Goes to a good cause."

I nodded, mentioned I'd think it over and steered him back to the house. I had learned years ago never to eat anything that began with cat or ended with rat.

My only experience with a plate full of muskrat in Smyrna a few years before had been less than satisfying, but unforgettable. If I closed my eyes, I could still see the little brown paw hanging over the side of the stained tan plastic bowl. So I had no plans to attend the shindig, even if the tickets were free. But I didn't want Gus to think I was ignoring him, so I lied.

"I'll check my schedule and might give you a call, but if not, don't hold them for me. It'll be my loss."

"Damn right!" he said, nodding and then shoved the tickets back into his shirt pocket.

"Now, about this ghost house," I said, again leading him toward our original focus.

"Yeah. The old house," Gus said, dropping his thin frame back onto a set of wooden steps. "Oh, my, yes. Well, as far as I remember, the first inklin' of unusual activity was that young woman up in the second-floor winda. Used to be a master bedroom they says. This good-looking young thing, with long brown hair, used to stand in the winda and comb out them long locks with a brush. Real slow like. She'd stand there a good long time," Gus said. "So long that people walkin' by would stop an' notice. Then they'd tell somebody else an' ask, 'Ya see that young thing up in the winda at the old Smithers' place?' An' some would say back, 'Yeah. I seened 'er,' or 'No. I ain't, but I'll keep watchin'. Is she a looker?' An' when word got out she was a real good looker for sure, why them boys in town—young an' old ones—they'd just park them behinds acrosst' street and wait for her to show up an' appear. Sorta like a drive-in movie show, without no cars, just fellas lined up in a row, waitin' to start watchin'."

Ghosts

Gus said there was one humorous incident involving the mystery woman.

"Ya know, one of the fellas workin' in town, a 'lectric meter reader I think it was. He'd been thinkin' 'bout her an' he even tried to ask her out on a date. Wanted to take her out, he did. He said he knocked an' knocked on her door, rung the bell, but she wouldn't answer. Figured she was playin' hard to get."

Eventually, Gus said, the landlord heard the stories that were circulating around town and became concerned. He stopped the young lady with blond hair, who was the official apartment renter, and demanded to meet her roommate. Of course, Gus said, the girl had no idea what the landlord was talking about.

"Claimed she didn't have no roommate, but everybody knew she was lyin'."

But Gus said the landlord told the woman it didn't matter if there was a roommate The rent would not go up, he just wanted to know the brown-haired girl's name. Still the young woman denied what everyone in the neighborhood knew to be a fact. There was a mysterious brown-haired resident living in that apartment.

After the first-floor tenant, who lived below the mystery lady, reported that he had heard the sounds of footsteps and music coming from the apartment above—during the day when the blond haired tenant of record was at work—the landlord and a group of witnesses entered the second-floor dwelling.

"They went through the whole damn place," Gus said, "every room an' closet door was opened an' checked an' rechecked. They found nothin' at all. They came up empty handed. It was damn furstratin' for sure. But, soon after that the apparitions in the winder was gone for good. Ruined the free entertainment, they did, with their pokin' around. Some folks, especially the young boys, was real upset."

Not too much later, the blond-haired tenant moved out. No one knows if she was annoyed by the accusations or if something happened in her apartment that she didn't want to share.

"We'll never know for sure," Gus said. "They say the landlord found the place empty an' her key an' envelope with rent money on the middle of the floor one day. No forwardin' address. No nothin'. Gone in a flash, with no explanation."

The next incidents involved a tenant in the first floor apartment which had seen a more than fair amount of turnover in occupancy, so much so that folks began thinking that the brown-haired ghost girl must have moved to the ground floor.

"One night, in the middle of winter," Gus said, "the town police officer was makin' his rounds, an' he found this fella sleepin' in the back seat of his car, with the engine an' heater runnin' to keep hisself warm. The Chevy was parked right on the side of the haunted house."

When the officer asked for identification, the car's occupant said he would go inside and get the documents from his apartment, but only if the officer would accompany him. Aware of the strange stories associated with the building, the officer asked if something unusual had occurred that caused the man to decide to sleep in his car.

Immediately, the man began to tell the police officer about the lovely woman he had found lying in his bed when he returned home late the previous evening.

"He said she had silky brown hair and looked like a real beauty, an' she was fast asleep,' Gus said. "The fella thought he had died and went to heaven. He was feelin' no pain after a long night at the bar, an' wasn't in the mood to ask how an' why this nice young thing had done picked his stable to spend the night. Like I said, on account of the booze, reason an' common sense had departed this fella quite a bit earlier. Anyway, he told the cop that when he turned his surprise sleepin' beauty over, he said her face looked like a movie monster. Like the kind they had in them old black-an'-white, 1950s sci-fi pictures at the neighborhood movie house. All hairy lookin', with gray and black fish scales acrosst her face, an' a pig snout for a nose. He sobered up real fast, right then. Jumped back, pulled his hands away like they touched hot coals an' headed out the door. Didn't look back to see if she was a comin' after him or still in his bed.

"That fella was scared to death, he was. An' you and me would be, too. So, when the cop went into the apartment, 'course there was no one there. The cop signaled the fella to follow, an' he went on in, got his papers an' stuff an' went back out into the car for the rest of the night. He told the cop, 'I'm movin' outta here real soon!' By week's end, why he was long gone. An' I doubt he's been back in town here since."

Gus said two guys moved in next. They told the landlord they were aware of the ghost stories, but weren't concerned.

Ghosts

Since they weren't believers, no ghosts would appear. They said only believers could be affected by the spirits. Whatever came their way, they would handle it logically.

They did, for about two weeks. Then they were gone, but not before they mentioned to another tenant that they had seen the apparition of a young girl floating across their bedroom.

"I know this sounds crazy," Gus said, "but it got to be sorta fun to guess about how long folks would stay in the old place. We used to take up little side bets, few dollars, an' put it in a pot. We'd guess like if they would last less than two weeks, from two weeks to a month, then from a month to three. Amusin' it was. Didn't matter if ya won or not, just somethin' to pass the time.

"While I don't know the names of the folks or the exact incidents that drove 'em all out, I can tell ya, for damn certain, there was a lotta activity at that old place. Somebody always headin' in or outta them first- and second-floor 'partments."

After three more couples broke their one-year leases over a brief nine-month period, the owners convinced a minister to conduct a cleansing of the building—concentrating on the two active apartments.

Accompanied at midnight by a dozen of the landlord's relatives and friends, the preacher—clothed in black and holding a prayerbook and waving burning incense—led the group through the vacant apartments that were considered to be most active.

Of course, Gus said, the owners did their best to keep the rest of the building's tenants in the dark about the cleansing ceremony.

"No sense gettin' the rest of the payin' customers aggravated," Gus said. Then he smiled and let out a quick laugh, adding, "Like they was ignorant and feeble minded, not knowin' there was big problems in 1-A an' 2-A, right under their noses. I mean, with all that fast comin' an' goin' happenin' all the time they woulda have t' been deaf, dumb, blind and dead to not have some inklin'."

Gus paused to let that message sink in, then smiled and continued. "They say the group of 'em found them a nest," Gus said. "That's what they called it, 'a nest of evil spirits' in one of them far back closet corners. Said that was the source of the bad luck, right in there at that, whatever they called it—portal, I think it was. Place where them demons fly in an' out, sorta like a underground spirit subway station, a secret entrance an' exit for restless souls. They threw a lotta incense smoke and prayers in that direction, but it didn't do no good at that time. Just got the monsters upset's what I heard.

"One of the folks that was there said they all gotta real cold chill after they got done prayin' an' blowin' sweet smoke in the demon corner. Told me that the room got so cold they could see their breaths, like bein' outside in Jan'awary, but it was a hot sticky summer night. Ain't natural for that to happen like that. No way. Anyway, that was the end of the exorcism or whatever, The cleansin's what they called it. Then, few days went by, an' all of a sudden, they got no more reports of activity. Like it was over, just like that. Nothin', like it was all done. The demons had left the buildin'."

For the next two years, the entire apartment building was calm, and all reports of unusual events ceased. Tenants no longer carried their moving boxes out of the building within a few weeks of their arrival.

Life was much more normal than it had been for years. And that in itself was eerie.

"It was like they was playin' with us," Gus said. "Most of the town folks thought it was over, but I knew better. I knew they was just waitin' to come back, make a statement."

Apparently, Gus was correct. In this haunted house, as in others, evil never rests and only bides its time to reappear. Two events occurred within the span of a week.

First, the house was sold and moved to a lot the new owner thought would show off its charm and provide more parking. Plus, he had municipal approval to build an addition to increase the number of apartments and his revenue. He also planned to erect a new contemporary structure on the haunted home's original location.

"Come in an' picked the whole thing up and moved it 'bout four blocks away," Gus said. "Was big time entertainment for sure. Half the city was out watching them brace the old house up an' roll 'er down the street. Major league production.

"Folks was wonderin' if the ghosts stayed at the first property, on the land, or went for the ride with the old place when it moved," Gus said. "Coulda gone either way."

Ghosts

They soon found out the answer.

Six days after the house was in place, a sudden fire in 1-A, the first-floor haunted apartment with the fishscale beauty, burned the entire dwelling to the ground. It was a miracle there were no injuries.

Although the apartment where the blaze had begun—and the entire house—was vacant at the time, the fire marshal stated that the cause was a lit antique oil lamp that had tipped over.

"It started in the middle of a hot, sunny afternoon, when the place was all empty," Gus said. "Don't make no sense. If there was nobody livin' in there at all, what was an ol' kerosene lamplight doin' in there in the first place? An', on toppa that, why was it even lit? Don't figure. There's just two answers."

I waited for Gus to share his thoughts.

He smiled, and looked at me, then said, "You want me to say it, doncha?"

"Of course," I replied, nodding and closing my notebook.

"Kids causin' mischief is one."

"Makes sense, especially if you're looking for a logical explanation," I said, agreeing. "And the other?" I asked, playing his game.

"The demon from the closet musta come back to kill off the house for good. That's the one I'd place my bet on," he said, firmly. "The way I figured it, that evil spirit was calm and quiet, waitin' us out. But he couldn't hold off for too long, 'cause he needed a little excitement. So, he come on back in through that closet porthole, an' started the inferno. Maybe he didn't like the new view after they moved his old place. Who will ever know? All I know is, he rose up an' finished the ol' place off once an' for all, an' went out in a blaze o' glory. That's the best answer I can give ya. Whattaya think?"

"I think you're right, Gus. I think you're right."

But Gus added one final issue to the mix, "Sometimes, if I walk down the street where that haunted house was at first, I'll sorta look up at that new place they built there an just stare. Can't help wonderin' if maybe it's back. An' I ain't the only one. Few others'll take a gander an' expect to see that brown-haired girl a lookin' out that winder, like before."

Then he paused, waved his hand as if what he was about to say was too silly to share, not worth speaking aloud.

"Go ahead," I said, urging him on.

Responding, Gus shook his head and laughed, adding, "Okay. See. What if it, or the girl or whatever, burned up the old place, like I said. An' then, it headed right on back to its old stompin' grounds. Hell, who knows what's under that foundation or property? Could be some of them old Johnny Reb ghosts that they buried all over the town to hide from the Yanks. Or coulda been an old Indian ritual ground, or even a murder mighta been at the old place, or a dead baby or two that somebody had in secret an' hid in the yard so nobody would find outta 'bout it. Could be a dozen strange happenin's that we don't know about an' never will. Whatever the cause, maybe it's back—that evil demon spirit—where it feels good, comfortable."

"Makes sense," I said, agreeing and thanking him for sharing his opinion.

Gus nodded, stood up, indicating the interview was over. I told him he had shared a lot of "real good stuff." He liked that, and he was pleased when I added that he was my new primary source for folklore and ghost stories in DC. I also promised to change his name in the story and never reveal his real identity.

"Sorta makes me a secret agent of sorts," he said, smiling. "I like that."

Then, after he gave me directions so I could drive by the "new" home that had been built on the old haunted site, he leaned in my car window and added, "Guess it looks sorta strange to them newcomers that moved in there."

"How so?" I replied.

For them to look outta their winders," Gus said, snickering, "an' see a buncha locals outside gazin' at their house like that. But, who cares? Ya gotta expect strange things like that in small towns. After all, with us movin' at a slower pace, we gotta lot less distractions an' plenty o' time to notice a lot more things than you city folks do, 'specially haunts. You got 'em, too. You just don't know 'em, don't notice 'em, like we do."

Ed and Kathleen Okonowicz

Ed Okonowicz, a Delaware native, is an editor and writer at the University of Delaware, where he also teaches both storytelling and feature writing classes. Kathleen Burgoon Okonowicz, a watercolor artist and illustrator, is originally from Greenbelt, Maryland, and is an artist member of the Baltimore Watercolor Society.

Photo by Bob Cohen

A professional storyteller, Ed presents programs throughout the Mid-Atlantic region. He is a member of the Delaware Humanities Forum Speakers Bureau and Visiting Scholars Program and has served on the Maryland State Arts Council Traditional/Folk Arts Advisory Panel.

Kathleen enjoys taking things of the past and preserving them in her paintings. Her print, *Special Places*, features the stately stairway in Wilmington, Delaware, that was the "special place" of the characters in Ed's love story, *Stairway over the Brandywine*. In the fall of 1999, she released *Station No. 5,* a print that captures the charm of a 1893 Victorian-style firehouse also in Wilmington, near Trolley Square.

A graduate of Salisbury State University, Kathleen earned her master's degree in professional writing from Towson State University. In addition to painting, she teaches a self-publishing course at the University of Delaware.

As the owners of Myst and Lace Publishers Inc., Kathleen is responsible for art, photography, layout and design, while Ed conducts the interviews and writes the stories.

**For information on storytelling, call Ed. For self-publishing or graphic design assistance, call Kathleen.
Telephone: 410 398-5013.**

Myst and Lace Publishers

Myst and Lace Publishers, Inc. was formed in 1994 during an early evening neighborhood walk. I mentioned to Kathleen that I needed to find a "few more" local ghost stories to use during my storytelling programs. I had been buying books about ghosts and folklore featuring stories in other states and I said, "I bet if we placed a notice that I was seeking ghost stories in the local newspapers, we might get two or three responses."

Within a week of the appearance of headlines in several newspapers stating: "Guy Wants Ghosts," we received more than 24 letters and phone calls from people with tales to tell. The result was *Pulling Back the Curtain*, Vol. I of the Spirits Between the Bays ghost/folklore series. As the years passed, we kept receiving leads—through the mail, over the phone and at book signing and storytelling events. The series, whose titles led readers through our literary haunted house, continued: through the open Door, into the Vestibule, and Parlor, and Kitchen, up the Back Stairway, into the Hallway and ending in the Bedchamber (with Vol. IX).

Along the way, our friend John Klisavage, owner of Washington Street Books and Antiques in Havre de Grace, Md., led us into the fascinating world of haunted antiques—resulting in two volumes about *Possessed Possessions*.

Our company's proudest achievement came in the summer of 1997, with the release of *Disappearing Delmarva: Portraits of the Peninsula People*. This hardbound, coffeetable-style book with photographs and stories, received two national first-place awards (in both the general book and the photography catagories). During its production, we were honored to meet the wonderful people who live on the peninsula and contribute to its distinct regional culture, traditions and folkways.

We've also produced two murder mystery novels—*FIRED!* and *Halloween House*—set in the fictional state of DelMarVa, featuring "tough on crime" governor Henry McDevitt and police commissioner Michael Pentak. This series and its characters will continue.

Terryfing Tales of the Beaches and Bays and *Ghosts* are our newest books, both released in 2001. We have plans to expand our output in the near future.

Ghosts

If you are one of our long-time readers, look for the new *Ghosts* series to continue. For those who enjoyed *Disappearing Delmarva*, a sequel is half completed and on its way, and our mystery readers will enjoy more local mayhem in *HOSTAGE*, DelMarVa Murder Mystery #3.

We also have agreed to publish the book of a local historian on a Delmarva subject, are working on a biography and are reviewing other works by regional authors for possible publication.

Since in 1994, Myst and Lace Publishers has focused on regional topics that both entertain and educate our readers to the history, folklore, culture and legends of our area. In each of our books, whether they focus on ghosts, murder or folklore, our readers learn interesting facts about Delmarva's past, and this is what we intend to continue in the future.

To those of you who have supported us, we thank you. If you are a new reader, welcome to our DelMarValous world. Also, plan to visit us on our web site [mystandlace.com] for the lastest details about our books and events. It should be operational in the middle of September 2001.

—Ed Okonowicz
in Fair Hill, Maryland,
at the northern edge
of the Delmarva Peninsula
—Fall 2001

MYST AND LACE PUBLISHERS

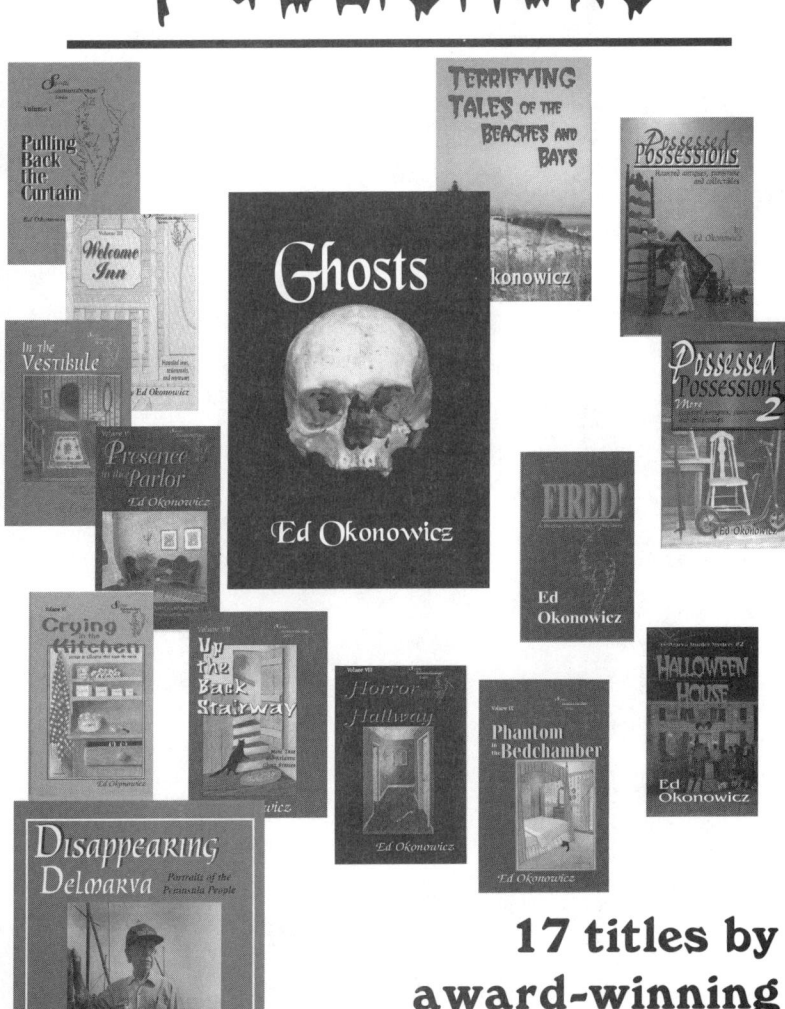

17 titles by award-winning author Ed Okonowicz

POSSESSED OBJECTS PLAGUE THEIR OWNERS

112 pages
5 1/2" x 8 1/2"
softcover
ISBN 0-9643244-5-8

112 pages
5 1/2" x 8 1/2"
softcover
ISBN 0-890690-02-3

$9.95 each

A BUMP. A THUD. MYSTERIOUS MOVEMENT. Unexplained happenings. Caused by What? Venture through this collection of short stories and discover the answer. Experience 20 eerie, true tales about items from across the country that, apparently, have taken on an independent spirit of their own—for they refuse to give up the ghost.

From Maine to Florida, from Pennsylvania to Wisconsin . . haunted heirlooms exist among us . . . everywhere.

Read about them in *Possessed Possessions* and *Possessed Possessions* **2** the books some antique dealers *definitely* do not want you to buy.

> "If you're looking for an unusual gift for a collector of antiques, or enjoy haunting tales, this one's for you."
> —Collector Editions

> "This book is certainly entertaining, and it's even a bit disturbing."
> —Antique Week

> ". . . an intriguing read."
> —Maine Antique Digest

WARNING
There could be more than just dust hovering around some of the items in your home.

---

www.mystandlace.com

. . . and you thought sharks were the only danger at the beach!

In *Terrifying Tales of the Beaches and Bays*, award-winning author and storyteller Ed Okonowicz shares eerie accounts of spirits roaming the shore.

Read about:

- A river pilot's memorable New Year's Eve cruise
- Desperate Confederates escaping from an island prison
- Serious seekers of pirate gold
- Fishermen stranded in the icy Chesapeake Bay
- Lighthouse keepers still tending long-gone beacon
- A most unusual "catch of the day"
- Ocean City's "Trash Rat"
- and more . . . .

A Delmarva beach-reading best seller in 2001

128 pages
5 1/2" x 8 1/2"
softcover
ISBN 1-890690-06-6
$9.95

www.mystandlace.com

True Ghost Stories from Master Storyteller Ed Okonowicz

Spirits Between the Bays Series

Volume by volume our haunted house grows. Enter at your own risk!

Wander through the rooms, hallways and dark corners of this eerie series.

Creep deeper and deeper into terror, and learn about the area's history in our series of ghostly tales and folklore of the Mid-Atlantic region.

"If this collection doesn't give you a chill, check your pulse, you might be dead."
—Leslie R. McNair
The Review, University of Delaware

"This expert storyteller can even make a vanishing hitchhiker story fresh and startling."
—Chris Woodyard
author of Haunted Ohio series

Pulling Back the Curtain
Spirits Between the Bays series—Vol. I

The first book of the 13-volume *Spirits Between the Bays* ghost/folkore series includes more than a dozen Mid-Atlantic ghost tales, including the curse of Blackbeard's Treasure, the Revolutionary War's Headless Horseman of Welsh Tract Road and the Ghost of Ashley Manor.

"In Pulling Back the Curtain by Ed Okonowicz, the Cecil County resident doesn't have to go far to find ghosts." —Baltimore Sun

"The stories are even more fascinating for local readers because Okonowicz interviewed Delmarva residents for the book." — Cecil Whig [Elkton, Md.]

"Okonowicz collects, refines and tells interesting legends and folk tales that have been passed by families from generation to generation." —Newark Post [Newark, Del.]

www.mystandlace.com

Opening the Door
Spirits Between the Bays series—Vol. II

This volume includes 13 true tales, including the ghosts of Woodburn, Delaware's Governor's Mansion, Elmer Tyson: Eastern Shore Gravedigger, the Bleeding Stone of White House Farm, a spirit-infested mobile home, restless souls at a Delaware River oil refinery and more.
(This volume is temporarily out of print, but will be reissued soon.)

Welcome Inn
Spirits Between the Bays series—Vol. III

Storytelling World
Honor Award

Welcome Inn series features true stories of unusual events at 13 public sites—including restaurants, inns and museums—visited by people every day. We invite the daring, the curious and especially the skeptics, to take a spirited trip across the peninsula--from the Chadds Ford Inn in Pennsylvania, to the Blue Coat Inn in Dover, to a pair of haunted inns in Snow Hill, Maryland, and in Fort Delaware's Civil War dungeons . . . plus other sites. Make your reservations to dine at a haunted table, stay overnight in a ghost room or tour a mysterious museum. Who knows what chills you will experience . . . what phantoms you will meet?

". . . *a sort of auto-club guide to ghosts, spirits and the unexplainable by Ed Okonowicz, a free-lance writer and ghost junkie.*" — Washington Times/Associated Press

In the Vestibule
Spirits Between the Bays series—Vol. IV

This book includes 15 true tales about a wide range of unusual creatures, including haunted horses at a thoroughbred stable on Maryland's Eastern Shore, a ghost infested hotel in New Jersey, Bigfoot's visits to Maryland, sightings of the Snallygaster, Delmarva's first serial killer, the notorious Patty Cannon, and many more.

From Avalon and Ocean City in New Jersey, to Lewes and Wilmington in Delaware and in Baltimore, Reliance and Easton in Maryland, the dead still walk at night.

*Delaware Press Association
First Place Award
1997*

"If this collection doesn't give you a chill, check your pulse, you might be dead."
— The Review [University of Delaware]

"The 15 stories, mostly creepy, in In the Vestibule, include one about Patty Cannon..."
— Star Democrat [Easton, Md.]

*Delaware Press Association
First Place Award
1998*

Presence in the Parlor
Spirits Between the Bays series—Vol. V

Features 19 true ghost stories and two popular legends. The chapters include tales of haunted Indian sites, ghosts in Baltimore Harbor on the USS Constellation, a floating casket that comes home to rest in Accomack County, Va., ghost stories from Tangier Island, the "Dream Lady" in Talbot County, Md., and haunted inns in New Castle, Del., and Salem, N.J.

"Okonowicz lulls the reader into a false sense of security and then—Wham!—he hits you with some terrifying detail..." — Chris Woodyard, Invisible Ink

"So make some hot chocolate, turn out the lights, light some candles and read this local ghost story aloud." — The Sentinel-Ledger [Ocean City, N.J.]

Crying in the Kitchen
Spirits Between the Bays series—Vol. VI

This book focuses on ghost stories based on interviews with residents of Mid-Atlantic water-towns—such as Cape May, Lewes, Chincoteague, Salem, New Hope and Rehoboth Beach. Read about the headless phantom on Smith Island in the Chesapeake Bay and learn about ghosts featured on the evening Lantern Tours at the old Civil War prison at Fort Delaware on Pea Patch Island. Discover details on the submerged city of Conowingo, the Weather Witch that protects a sunken treasure ship, the Unknown Sailors' Cemetery under the Lewes Ferry Terminal parking lot and the mass graves of Confederate prisoners at Fort Mott National Cemetery. . . and more.

"...when the lights go down, just remember, watch out for what is—or isn't—behind you!"
— Delaware River and Bay Authority Traveler

"Hidden slaves left to die in a secret passage, a Lewes parking lot built over a graveyard..."
— Dover Post [Dover, Del.]

"Okonowicz's new book is much different than the others in that it highlights only 'coast ghosts'."
— Beachcomber [Ocean City, Md.]

Delaware Press Association
Second Place Award
2000

Up the Back Stairway
Spirits Between the Bays series—Vol. VII

This book features 26 stories of Mid-Atlantic haunts, including demonic spirits in Salem County, N.J., ghosts in Pennsylvania's Red Rose Inn and strange events in Virginia's Oak Spring Farm, plus the legend of the Ticking Tomb, mysterious melodies from Fiddler's Bridge, ghostly pirates on the Jersey Shore, a vampire tale set on the Eastern Shore of Maryland. . . and more.

"DON'T read these stories alone, late at night, in the dead of winter, when no one can hear your screams." — Port Deposit Post [Port Deposit, Md.]

www.mystandlace.com

Horror in the Hallway
Spirits Between the Bays series—Vol. VIII

Terror awaits at every page turn as readers progress through this eighth volume of the *Spirits Between the Bays* ghost/folklore series. These 28 tales are from people living in Pennsylvania, Maryland, New Jersey and Delaware. All have experienced the unexplained and share their stories about the curse of a deadly violin, the evil occupant of an antique bed, a jinxed bungalow, the haunted jail in Denton, Md., restless slave ghosts in a Pennsylvania farmhouse and the long hidden horror associated with the Pink House. . . . and more.

Delaware Press Association
First Place Award
2000

Phantom in the Bedchamber
Spirits Between the Bays series Vol. IX

Civil War ghosts and haunted lighthouses are the focus of this volume. Learn of the spirits in Gettysburg's Farnsworth House Inn and Restaurant and the ghosts at Point Lookout State Park (at one time site of the Nation's Largest Civil War Prison).

Readers also will encounter and enjoy eerie tales associated with a graveyard near Easton, Maryland, ghostly activity in two Delaware businesses, ghost hunters in New Jersey, what it's like to move a corpse and the strange encounters at "the most haunted lighthouse in America," located at the southern tip of Maryland's Western Shore.

Nearly 20 stories are included in this terrifying volume, and eight of the sites are open to the public--the most listed in any volume since Welcome Inn, Vol. III, our very popular book on haunted inns restaurants and museums.

Stairway over the Brandywine
A Love Story

Two people meet during World War II, fall in love, and make a pledge on a stairway overlooking the Brandywine River. Can their love survive the war?

Meet Bill, an Army Air Corps pilot, and Jean, a small town girl, who meet in the early days of World War II. Like scenes from a 1940s movie, they fall in love, make a commitment and are separated by the war. Here is a good, old-fashioned, sentimental love story that is ideal for the young-at-heart of any generation.

24 pages
5 1/2" x 8 1/2"
softcover
ISBN 0-9643244-2-3
$5.00

Treasure Hunting
Seek and You Shall Find

by
Eddie Okonowicz

Loaded with
- tips on using a metal detector to hunt for treasure, and
- photos of numerous historical finds

$6.95 plus
$1.50 for shipping

- Authorized dealer of new and used metal detectors and treasure hunting equipment and accessories
- Lost and Found assistance
- 15 years experience in the field

To order copies of the book, or for information on metal detectors, public presentations and school programs, contact:

Eddie Okonowicz, 125 East Delaware Canal Court,
Middletown, Delaware 19709   (302) 376-3887

www.mystandlace.com

The DelMarVa Murder Mystery series

320 pages
4 1/4" x 6 3/4"
softcover
ISBN 1-890690-01-5
$9.95

FIRED!

Early in the 21st century, DelMarVa, the newest state in the union, which includes Delaware and the Eastern Shore of Maryland and Virginia, is plagued by a ruthless serial killer. In FIRED! meet Gov. Henry McDevitt, Police Commissioner Michael Pentak and State Psychologist Stephanie Litera as they track down the peninsula's worst killer since 19th century murderess Patty Cannon.

WELCOME to the State of DelMarVa

"Politics and romance make fairly strange bedfellows, but add a dash of mystery and mahem and the result can be spectacular, as evidenced in FIRED!"
—Sharon Galligar Chance
BookBrowser Review

"Lots of familiar places in this imaginative suspense novel."
—Jeannine Lahey
About.com
Wilmington, Del.

". . . this is Okonowicz's best book so far!"
—The Star Democrat
Easton, Md.

320 pages
4 1/4" x 6 3/4"
softcover
ISBN 1-890690-03-1
$9.95

Halloween House

In Halloween House, the series continues as Gov. McDevitt, Commissioner Pentak and other DelMarVa crime fighters go up against Craig Dire, a demented businessman who turns his annual Halloween show into a real-life chamber of horrors.

Delaware Press Association
First Place Award
2000

"Halloween House mystery chills summer heat."
—Rosanne Pack
Cape Gazette

"Looking at the front cover, the reader knows it's going to be a bumpy night."
—Erika Quesenbery
The Herald

www.mystandlace.com

Disappearing Delmarva
Portraits of the Peninsula People

Photography and stories by Ed Okonowicz

Disappearing Delmarva introduces you to more than 70 people on the peninsula whose professions are endangered. Their work, words and wisdom are captured in the 208 pages of this hardbound volume, which features more than 60 photographs.

Along the back roads and back creeks of Delaware, Maryland, and Virginia—in such hamlets as Felton and Blackbird in Delaware, Taylors Island and North East in Maryland, and Chincoteague and Sanford in Virginia—these colorful residents still work at the trades that have been passed down to them by grandparents and elders.

208 pages
8 1/2" x 11"
Hardcover
ISBN 1-890690-00-7

$38.00

Winner of 2 First-Place Awards:

Best general book
Best Photojournalism entry

National Federation of Press Women Inc.
1998 Communication Contest

Ed presents a program based on this award-winning book at local historical societies and libraries. Contact him at 410 398-5013 to arrange a program in your area.

www.mystandlace.com

To complete your collection. . .
or to tell us about *your* ghostly experience, use the form below:

Name _____

Address_____

City_____State_____Zip Code_____

Phone Numbers _(_____)_____(_____)_____
                                Day   Evening

To receive the free *Spirits Speaks* newsletter and information on future volumes, visit our web site [www.mystandlace.com] or fill out the above form and mail it to us.

I would like to order the following books:

Quantity	Title	Price	Total
_____	**Ghosts**	$ 9.95	_____
_____	Terrifying Tales of the Beaches and Bays	$ 9.95	_____
_____	Pulling Back the Curtain, Vol I	$ 8.95	_____
_____	Opening the Door, Vol II (temporarily out of print)		_____
_____	Welcome Inn, Vol III	$ 8.95	_____
_____	In the Vestibule, Vol IV	$ 9.95	_____
_____	Presence in the Parlor, Vol V	$ 9.95	_____
_____	Crying in the Kitchen, Vol VI	$ 9.95	_____
_____	Up the Back Stairway, Vol VII	$ 9.95	_____
_____	Horror in the Hallway, Vol VIII	$ 9.95	_____
_____	Phantom in the Bedchamber, Vol IX	$ 9.95	_____
_____	Possessed Possessions	$ 9.95	_____
_____	Possessed Possessions 2	$ 9.95	_____
_____	Fired! A DelMarVa Murder Mystery(DMM)	$ 9.95	_____
_____	Halloween House DMM#2	$ 9.95	_____
_____	Disappearing Delmarva	$38.00	_____
_____	Stairway over the Brandywine, A Love Story	$ 5.00	_____
_____	Treasure Hunting (See ordering information on page 103.)		

*Md residents add 5% sales tax.
Please include $2.00 postage for the first book, and 50 cents for each additional book.
Make checks payable to:
Myst and Lace Publishers

Subtotal_____
Tax*_____
Shipping_____
Total_____

All books are signed by the author. If you would like the book(s) personalized, please specify to whom.

                      Mail to: Ed Okonowicz
                      1386 Fair Hill Lane
                      Elkton, Maryland 21921

                      www.mystandlace.com